Well, Fare Thee Well

Mitch Norman is a popular musician and songwriter in West Dorset. He is a DJ and an enthusiastic record collector of soul music. He has made several recordings of acoustic music and has played guitar in local groups and now performs as a solo artist. Mitch is also a painter in a naive style and has exhibited his work. This is his first book, written some years ago and left in a drawer in his garage until recently rediscovered.

Published in 2013 by FeedARead.com Publishing –
Arts Council funded

A CIP catalogue record for this title is available from
the British Library.

WELL, FARE THEE WELL

MITCH NORMAN

With many thanks to Margery, Hadassah and Helen for
all their help in publishing this book

Front cover illustration: Mitch Norman
Back cover photo: Richard Smith
Scooter drawings: Bill

Dedicated to
Skinny, Bill and the crew of '71
Once a mod, always a mod.

Part I

First Horizon

Chapter 1

The mizzle that had continued throughout the evening developed suddenly into a drenching downpour five minutes after the Picture House had turned out its few occupants, and we were caught in its unexpected fury.

By the time we had ridden from the traffic lights down to our refuge in the fish and chip shop, we were as sodden as water rats. The interior of the place warmed us slightly as we queued along the aluminium counter, but once our chips were purchased, back out into the cold, stinging rain we had to go.

We waited in the fish and chip shop doorway and watched the rain form puddles on the tarmac, then decided that we couldn't go home yet. The car park was deserted apart from a couple of empty cars parked by the far wall. A police car hidden behind the toilets swung out into the car park, circled around and sizzled passed us. The two policemen who occupied the vehicle eyed us with bored expressions. But the weather was on our side that night; they drove past and soon disappeared around the corner. Spot-checks were dreaded and frequent in those days. I exhaled a sigh of relief; I had two bald tyres and couldn't afford to buy new ones.

Alex, the tallest amongst us, blond haired, attired like an urban gypsy-dandy gone to seed and who was always short of money, unwrapped his chips and began eating hungrily. Matthew, the oldest in the crowd, like a snow-walking, lumbering bear wrapped in his great-coat, blew on his hands, then grumbled that he had left his gloves at home. His long black curly hair was like an unruly judge's wig, his expression more mature and knowing than the rest of us, a long dark scarf tied tightly around his thick neck.

There were five of us that night, but as it was Monday, cold, wet and uncomfortable, five wasn't really a bad number. We had just been to the pictures, as we did every Monday, but that night the film had been particularly bad; a French offering with English subtitles.

'D'you ever find,' said Alex, throwing his finished chip-paper into the dustbin by the wall. 'That by the time you've read the words at the bottom of the screen, they change, so that you never see the film; all you do is read all that superimposed writing?'

'If you could read,' said Matthew. 'Perhaps you wouldn't find it such a struggle.'

'That's a good one,' I said.

'You've got to admit it, though, it was a pretty bad film,' said Gary, almost pretty, boyishly-beautiful with angelic curls, sky-blue eyes, who seemed to have a different girl every night, who was now cuddling and enveloping a voluptuously plump and pretty girl by the glass door.

'Probably the worst I've seen in my whole life,' Alex replied with a deep sigh.

'Anyway,' said Matthew, suddenly. 'It's stopped raining. I'm going home.'

He threw the remains of his chips into the dustbin and walked over to his scooter parked beneath the street lamp. The rain had subsided, and has lapsed into that ever-present drizzle. The sky appeared like a dark, murky expanse of drifting cobwebs. Matthew started his scooter, sat upon it, shifted into gear and rode up to us, shivering, his hands like lumps of red meat.

'See you lot tomorrow night,' he said, his voice a tone of bored expectancy.

9

We nodded.

Sure, we'd see him tomorrow night.

He hissed up the street, turned left at the junction, and was gone. The lights in the fish and chip shop flickered and went out, plunging us into darkness.

'Well,' said Gary, pulling himself from his cuddling, 'It's time we were going, too.'

He and his girlfriend stole one last lingering kiss, then walked over to the street lamp where our remaining scooters were parked. He started his scooter, sat upon it, beckoned his girl to mount on the back, selected gear and cruised up to us.

'See you lot tomorrow,' he said, and turning right at the junction, was gone.

Alex and I stood in the fish and chip doorway, watching the drizzling rain drift like gossamer across the high street lamp.

'I liked the bit when the husband came home and found his wife in bed with her lover,' I said, remembering the film.

'I didn't,' said Alex. 'I thought the film was a load of shit.'

I dug into my parka pocket and bought out a crushed, wet packet of cigarettes along with some pocket fuzz.

'Want one?' I asked.

Alex took a cigarette without speaking, produced a box of matches from his pocket and we lit up, coughing.

'Christ,' said Alex. 'What are these things made of, seaweed?'

'I've had them for over a week,' I said. 'I'm trying to give them up.'

'What made you start again?'

I shrugged my shoulders.

'I've given up trying to give up.' I explained.

Alex coughed again and grimaced.

'Christ, these are enough to make anybody want to give up smoking.'

The distant church clock chimed faintly with the time. It was quarter to eleven. Alex pulled another long drag from the cigarette and flicked it sideways into the gutter where it hissed and went out. An assistant from the fish and chip shop came from the side door, pulled his raincoat up around his neck, and walked past us.

'Goodnight, lads,' he said.

We nodded and said goodnight. A car came into the car park, circled around, and drove out again. A wet dog barked in a distant housing estate. Alex stepped over to the drink machine and inserted a five penny piece, waited, then pulled out a plastic cup of hot coffee.

'Want a sip?'

'No thanks,' I said.

Alex drank the steaming beverage quickly, slurping, and tossed the empty cup on the ground.

'Well,' he said, 'nothing's going to happen tonight. I may as well go home.'

He walked over to his blue Vespa, dirty, scruffy and undecorated beneath the street lamp. He started it up and sat upon it.

'Another day in our lives,' he said. 'In this eroding year of 1971. What's to become of us seventeen year old degenerates? What's tomorrow gonna bring? What's gonna happen, huh?'

He pondered, then frowned, darkly illuminated in the street-lamp, his scooter rattling and spluttering. Then he smiled weakly, sped up the street, jerking and backfiring, skidded slightly at the junction, and turning left, was gone. The moon was a crescent of dim yellow

11

in the streaming sky. I pondered, tied up my plimsoll-lace and wandered over to my scooter.

Chapter 2

On most evenings of the week, apart from Mondays and Sundays, our usual rendezvous was the town's Youth Club. This was a large building near the town centre that consisted of numerable rooms, inspired, equipped and financed by the County Council. In these rooms we pleasured ourselves with the delights of the three large table-tennis tables, a darts board, a trampoline, a 22-inch television, a dark cupboard bursting with photographic equipment, a bar where we glutted ourselves with Cokes, Mars Bars, and a workshop at the far end of the building where we could make repairs to our scooters.

The Club in those days was our fortress, our refuge on winter evenings, our warming shelter against the clawing rains and piling snows; our seclusion, reclusion, our private world in a forgotten universe, a snugly lit den, like a rabbit hole in the midst of a battlefield.

It was the bar we frequented the most. This was a large room arranged like a lounge bar in a public house, with armchairs for our leisure, and a juke box. Along one wall a counter had been constructed adjoining a small kitchen, where we could purchase our cups of tea and chocolate bars. Alcohol was forbidden in the place, and cigarettes were not sold over the counter. (But this did not deter our needs for the forbidden; our local pub was just along the street).

On one wall, beside the precious juke box, was the notice board, advertising the forthcoming dances and the Club's functions during the week. On the opposite wall, extensive and colourful, a portrait of a young girl had been painted by Alex, our own competent artist.

Enmeshed in the girl's wild hair, deeply-painted fishing boats were tangled and distant, portraying our closeness to the sea, or more probably, Alex's desultory state of thinking, or inability to maintain interest in any one venture. The girl's eyes were large and blue, almost Betty Boopien, and so sad-looking, so little-puppy-dog lost. With the light from the bare light bulb, the entire mural crinkled and buckled with a corrugation of light, if you looked at it sideways.

The painting had taken Alex over a month to complete and he regarded it as one of his greater works. But the entire concept of that wall had a sadder, personal side. The girl looked suspiciously like one of Alex's heart throbs, though he wouldn't admit it to us or even to himself.

The juke box, that throbbing, beating heart of loud sound when conversation died, was our god, coloured-light winking idol, graven image, golden-rhomboid calf, worshipped fervently and fed, kept alive, with five penny pieces.

We stood before it, reflected in its timeless layers of glass and chromium, selected our hymns and canticles, offered our humble gifts of silver, then returned to our pews to nod and pray to the rhythmic pulsation of the current Top Ten.

Three records were chosen and changed every two weeks so that we were always kept up-to-date and deafened. Yes. That silver, bulky, majestic mechanism was well-serviced and esteemed in our society; a raucous backcloth to the stage on which we expired those winter evenings of our youth.

And thus, to the foggy strains of Junior Walker's gilded saxophone...*What does it take...to win your love for me..?* our Tuesday evening began.

14

Matthew and I had arrived early and were sitting in the corner, by the door. I was smoking and Matthew was reading a *True Love* magazine. The girls collected these magazines and periodicals for our quiet moments. Matthew, not so enlightened by his particular page, closed the magazine and tossed it on a vacant chair beside him.

'It's surprising,' he said sighing, 'what shit these women read.'

The Club warden, a heavily bearded, garrulous non-stop talker whom we tried to avoid if humanly possible, came tripping from the staff office with some papers in his hand.

'Ah, boys,' he said, seeing us in that momentary unoccupied disposition. 'Do you want to join the new chess club? Every Wednesday in the spare room? Marvellous game. Most inspiring. I've ordered three new chess sets. We'll be holding a tournament and the winner could win a pound prize. Interested, Jack?'

I opened my mouth.

He continued. 'Great idea. We could even arrange to play against the neighbouring clubs. Great idea, right? Sign your names on the list on the notice board. I know you play chess, don't you Jack?'

I gaped.

'Well, I can play, but I'm not sure...'

'Marvellous,' said the warden, pushing his glasses up the bridge of his nose. 'Marvellous. The more the merrier. That's what I like about this Club; team spirit, the enthusiasm to all muck in and make a project a success, whatever it may be. Take the photography club, for instance. So far, twenty of us have joined, now they're turning out photographs like they were born into the job, people who didn't even know what a negative was.'

'Opposite from positive,' I said.

'Ah, I surmise you haven't yet joined the photography club,' said the warden.

'It was a joke.'

'All joking aside,' continued the warden, brushing away my witticism like a wisp of hair, 'this Club, with all its side-lines included, is an encouraging success. The Council's increasing our grants every month. Most promising.'

'It's just somewhere to go,' said Matthew blandly.

'But once you're here, isn't it nice to be able to do something constructive, to learn something? Take Peter over there, only a month ago he hadn't even seen a trampoline, now you should see him. He bounces and leaps, spins and twirls. Really competent. We're really proud of him.'

Peter, a thin, acned, tousle-haired lad, peeped up from the pages of a *Learn Trampoline* manual and smirked.

'And when we've enough money to start our gardening group,' the warden enthused, pleased at the thought of his newest project, 'you'll be able to grow your own tomatoes. Just think.'

We thought.

'And watercress?' said Matthew, suddenly.

'And radishes?' I added.

'And sweet peas? And Sweet Williams? And rhubarb? And turnips?'

'And even...and...even...marrows?'

'Ah lads,' replied the warden, taken in by our provocative keenness. 'I see you're both interested. Great. Marvellous. I'll put both your names down.'

He bustled out into the games room raving about 'team spirit' and the exuberance of liberated youth.

16

Matthew watched his departure from the corners of his eyes then guffawed, slapping his knees with his hands.

'But he's such a...pain.'

'He goes on and on and...'

'I know what it is,' said Matthew. 'I bet his wife doesn't talk to him...'

'And all those words are locked inside him waiting to come bursting out.'

'Yeah. Like diarrhoea. Well, sort of. It would be if he spoke through his ass.'

Matthew stood up and stepped over to the glinting juke box, inserted a five-penny piece, and selected some records. He returned and sat down next to me again. At that instant Raymond, Gary and Alex entered the room attired in their bulky, shapeless parkas and long, coloured scarves wrapped around their necks. They padded up to us with silent, plimsolled feet, and sat down beside us. Raymond took a chair by the wall and pulled it up closer. He sat down, facing me.

'Are you lot coming to Highchester?' he said, always one for discovering the hidden secrets of excitement on the outer fringes of the town.

'I can't,' I said. 'I've just joined the gardening group.'

'What?'

'He's joking,' said Matthew. 'What's on in Highchester?'

'Y'know. The cellar bar? Highchester Arms? Disco? Dancing? Girls?'

He spoke as though we might guess his train of thought by giving us a rapid, answerless questionnaire. 'Well? You gonna come?'

Matthew's first record suddenly filled the place with the melodic gliding glissando strings of the Motown orchestra.

'I'm not,' said Gary dogmatically. 'I'm gonna stay and knock off Sarah Trueman.'

'You won't do it,' said Matthew.

'Anyway. Who's coming?' said Raymond, losing his enthusiasm slightly. 'I'll go on my own.'

'Alright,' said Matthew. 'I'll come.'

'I will, if somebody takes me,' said Alex. 'I'm broke.'

'Alright. I'll take you,' said Raymond. 'You coming, Gary?'

Gary was gazing at Sarah Trueman, who had just walked in and was sitting cross-legged beside the juke box.

'No. I told you once I'm gonna...'

'Yeah. Alright. So that's four of us so far,' said Raymond, turning his head to look at Sarah Trueman. 'Shall we wait for more of us to arrive?'

'I can't go yet anyway,' said Matthew, tapping his foot on the tiled floor. 'I've got another two records to go on the juke box.'

Chapter 3

When only Owen arrived, and decided to come with us, the five of us left for Highchester. It was only sixteen miles away, but that night the road was blotted, concealed by a dark, thick, swirling fog. You could almost reach out and tear it away from around you, like soiled cotton wool. I had to strain my eyes to see, carefully following Raymond's dull-red, floating, bobbing, burning tail-light. Then it rained. When we finally reached Highchester we were soaking wet, and had headaches.

Highchester was considerably larger than our town, but the streets were just as sleepy and quiet; just another town shuttered and locked up for the night, secure, blanketed until the morning, and silent. The fog had lifted here, and a few lone walkers strolled along the dimly-lit pavements. We rode noisily down the high street. A tiny, trotting, mongroid dog turned its head as we passed. The larger shops had their windows brightly illuminated with stark yellow light.

Raymond, riding in front of us, as usual, coasted along the edge of the pavement, then stopped alongside the kerb. Alex, riding pillion, twisted his body around and waved us down. We stopped alongside them. Raymond pulled his scarf down from his lips.

'Christ. That fog. I could hardly see beyond my own nose.'

'It was like riding through a blanket,' said Owen, pulling off his gloves and rubbing his eyes.

'Yeah. So OK,' said Matthew, blipping his throttle. 'Let's just get to the disco, shall we?'

'Alright. Alright,' said Raymond, looking pained. 'It's only just up the street.'

Alex waved us on with his long arm.

'Onward, then, impatient boppers,' he cried. 'On you go to certain pandemonium.'

We sped on down the narrowing, darkening street, leaving Raymond and Alex still beside the pavement, waiting for a spluttering car to pass.

When we entered the Highchester Arms, the disco was already in full swing. As usual it was held in the large, spacious cellar bar, where the darkness and cobwebbed corners, the musty smells and dripping plaster, sagging ceiling, effulgence-raddled dance floor and festering aura all helped to add to the atmosphere. We worked our way over to the crowded bar. All age barriers seemed lifted, forgotten that evening. Older, burly workmen, as well as the younger sect were gathered together in their separate knots, glasses clenched in their fingers, gesticulating with their hands, shrieking and shouting above the music that surged and thumped about them like thick, loud eddies of syrup-gravy.

We reached the bar. I found a space, called to the barman, and bought a pint of bitter. I paid, sipped my drink, and looked about me. The disc jockey seemed to be working hard, bobbing and swaying behind his dual-decks, earphones clamped around his head, a record in his hand. He mumbled, growled into the stunted microphone, manipulated a box of dials and tricks, and as the music continued to bulge and swell, he assailed the place with darting, pelting lights, suddenly red, then blue, then yellow, then purple; a squall of sudden-shot pellets of bright, coloured light, splattering the dark, adobe walls with instant blobs of colour. He was full of tricks, it seemed.

Alex, having bought his vodka, came over and shouted in my ear.

'It's craziness, but shall we go and mingle?'

We worked our way through the crowd, still in our parkas, and stood by the throbbing wall. Raymond and Owen joined us. I gazed up and saw large, trembling, shiny bubbles slowly cascading down from a rotating, colander-like mechanism. It was like standing in some fantasy land.

'Hey,' Raymond shouted. 'They've got a live band.'

We looked over at the high stage. The disc jockey mumbled a further string of hushed words into his microphone, then stopped, pulling off his earphones. Beside him, a band was nervously tuning. The drummer was tapping his drums in abstracted bursts of inspiration. The three guitarists looked at each other. Were they ready? Yes, they were ready, all tuned, all tightly synchronized, well-rehearsed, raring to go, to entertain the heaving rabble they couldn't see in the noisy near-darkness. The disc jockey switched off his equipment. The band stepped forward into position, then commenced instantly with a loud raucous number that seemed to make the ceiling rumble.

Inspired, large lumps of girls began dancing in the corner. Urgent men, hotly attired in sharp suits and ties, ventured through the crowd to ask for partnership on the floor. The entire place was soon rocking and moiling around with sliding feet and nodding heads.

Alex, always the one for live music, began moving his body loosely, his left foot tapping the floor. Two girls, young and lithesome, slid through the crowd and appeared before us, dancing together. They were seduced and taken by the music, melting and moulding their bodies, rubbing their hips against the air from side to side, tight-jeaned bottoms wriggling, waggling, their arms punching upward. We watched as they slithered and smoothed their shapely bodies through every sensual, lustful motion. Raymond, without a word, stepped over, tapped one girl on the shoulder, and began dancing. Not being so adventurous, I downed my drink and went to the bar to buy another.

Waiting to be served, I gazed toward the exit door and my stomach turned cold. I saw Matthew surrounded by five shadowed youths in leather jackets, studded, twinkling with badges. My mind sparked alive with a single sudden fear...*greasers*.

I stood motionless, conscious of my parka. Then there was a scuffle and a clenched fist moved silently through the air. I heard a dull crack and Matthew fell limply to the floor. In a flustered state of panic I pushed back into the crowd. I reached Alex and pulled his parka sleeve.

'We've got trouble. Trouble. Matthew's just been floored by a gang of greasers.'

Alex looked at me and his eyes dilated.

'Oh shit.'

He reached over to Raymond, still dancing, and pulled him away. He toppled slightly, looked surprised, then angry. The two girls danced on, looking at us, puzzled.

'Wha...hey. What are you playing at?'

Alex shouted in his ear and he stood still, pondered, and then looked put-out.

'Balls,' he retorted. 'Can't we go bloody anywhere?'

'Where are they, for Chrissakes?' Alex asked me, a look of fear on his face.

'By the exit door,' I told him. 'What are we gonna do?'

Raymond shrugged his shoulders.

'C'mon, for Christ sake,' said Alex. 'He's our bloody mate. Well? Isn't he? We've gotta go and help him out.'

'Well. Go on, then. You go over there,' Raymond replied, knowing his solution wouldn't sell with the rest of us.

'God,' Alex snapped. 'What kind of friend are you?'

I stood shaking miserably, my mind desperately trying to focus on a plan of escape. Raymond's face went rapt and serious.

'C'mon,' he said.

There was now tenseness so thick in the loud air you could taste it. My stomach was melting, swirling with liquid frenzy. We reached the bar. We saw Matthew crumpled in the corner. We heard a loud, arrogant voice.

'Here's more of them nancy boys.'

A tall, gangling youth with unkempt hair, unshaven chin, dirty face and an earring lumbered over to me; came really close so that we were rubbing shoulders.

'Ere,' he whispered, his voice tinged with poison. 'D'you ride one of them little moddy things? I thought only women rode them.'

I looked into his face and his eyes shot into me with hatred.

'What if I do?' I asked.

Raymond pushed us apart.

'What did you hit our friend for?'

The youth stood rigid, taut, his fists clenching, his leather jacket squeaking.

'Don't touch me...you fucking nancy...'

Another youth, with the same apparel, as big as a bull, his chest bursting from his jacket, grabbed Raymond's shoulder.

'You been touching my mate...nancy?'

'I resent being called *nancy*,' said Raymond.

23

The situation was getting ludicrous. The blows would be coming any second. The barman stormed up to us.

'What the hell's going on here? I'm not having any trouble, d'you hear? Go on. Get out. All of you.'

The youth, built like a bull, grabbed Raymond by the collar and hurled him to the ground with a tearing sound.

'Hell,' the barman yelled. 'I'm going to call the police.'

He rushed off, pushing past a wide eyed girl who was watching and chewing gum. A crowd of people had gathered around us, and it was Alex and I against five greasers intent on spreading us upon the floor like crushed flies.

Owen was nowhere to be found. Raymond and Matthew had slunk off into the shadows like sodden cats. There was no sign of the bouncers. A woman screamed at us.

'Why don't you thugs go away? You're always causing trouble. Blasted hooligans.'

We stood there like absurd chess pieces, facing each other. Then I leapt, tripped, stumbled up and made for the door, followed by Alex who almost piled into me. We ran wildly down the cold, moon-bright gravel path, panting and cursing for our lives, and sped, weaving around cars, across the car park. I skidded along the gravel in a cloud of dust. The bull-youth had cut across the car park and we met, buffing each other slightly. He towered above me like a tree, panting, his immense chest heaving in and out, his voice rasping.

'You fucking...little runt...unless you apologise...for touching my friend...I'm going to…'

'Alright, alright, 'I gasped, weakly. 'I apologise. Anything to escape this ludicrous situation.'

'No,' he said, still panting, the badges on his leather lapels tinkling and twinkling in the moonlight, his fat, red face sneering. 'You've got to say it to my friend.'

He turned his head and bellowed across the car park.

'Tom. Over here. I've got one.'

Tom crunched over from the darkness. He reached us and made to hit me with clenched fist. I cowered, my arms hiding my face.

'Hang on, hang on,' said the bull-youth, pushing his friend away. 'He's gonna apologise.'

'I apologise,' I repeated. 'But it wasn't me who touched you.'

'I know it wasn't you,' said Tom, mimicking my voice spitefully. 'But you're gonna apologise anyway, for being a nancy boy.'

How I wished it had been anyone else and not me who had been caught. Where the hell were my 'friends', anyway?

'I apologise for being a nancy boy,' I replied, arduously.

'OK,' said the bull-youth. 'That's enough. Let's get going before the pigs get here.'

They shambled off into the dark. Alex and Owen, in opposite directions, popped up from behind car bonnets.

'Pssst. Jack. Have they gone yet?'

I leaned upon a car, breathing heavily, feeling wretched, small and defeated, listening to the rumble of motorcycles fading over the hill.

Chapter 4

One Friday night, being pay day, Alex and I both got very drunk, and very silly, and the warden banned us from the Club for a week. We spent the evening in the public house, and spent all our money. At closing time we stumbled out into the cold night air. I tripped slightly on the pavement, but kept my balance. Alex propped me up, and we started giggling. We walked carefully, dizzily, up the dark, swaying side-street. Alex belched softly beneath his breath.

'Did you ever realise what a bore Gary is?' he said, leaning against the red brick wall.

'How d'you mean?' I asked, feeling the air swelling all around me, pressing against my head.

'Dunno,' he replied. 'Something about him. Gets the women, though.'

'It's his aftershave.'

He hiccupped.

'Yeah. Sure. That's it,' he nodded, his face expressionless. 'It's the aftershave.'

'The Brut.'

'Yeah. Right. It's the aftershave.'

'Christ. I feel ill,' I groaned as the realisation suddenly hit me.

'C'mon you bum,' said Alex.

We turned the corner that led to the car park.

'We may as well meet the inevitable crowd at the usual hang-out.'

Our friends were at the far end of the car park, gathered around the drinks machine. We started walking across the vast, sweeping expanse of tarmac. Alex paused and zipped up his parka. It was getting colder.

'They're as predictable as shit,' he said, 'you can tell where they are by the time of day it is.'

He pulled a packet of cigarettes from his pocket, dropped it, and picked it up again. He offered me a cigarette. I declined. He lit up.

'I really feel like moving out of this hole of a town,' he said, shaking a match out.

'Gotta move away.'

'Where would you go?' I asked, as the night began to race around me.

'Brazil,' he said. 'It's hot there.'

'I couldn't go, anyway,' said Alex, pondering, cigarette smoke seeping from his mouth. 'My scooter wouldn't make it.'

We finally reached the crowd and I stood by the wall, feeling heavy.

'We thought you two would never make it across the car park without falling over,' said Matthew, grinning, eating chips.

'It was a long way to walk,' I said, holding on to the wall, fighting back slow, dull, upsurging feelings of sickness.

'Heard you two got chucked out of the club,' said Raymond.

'Who bloody cares,' said Alex, helping himself to Matthew's chips.

'There's plenty more places to go.'

'Yeah. That's right,' I said, wishing I could just crawl into bed or lie down, in a gutter, or anywhere.

'Mind you. It was pretty funny,' said Owen, 'when Jack blew that Durex up like a balloon and hung it from the ceiling.'

'Did I really do that?' I asked, shaking off the spasms of illness, momentarily.

'Right in the middle of the bar,' said Raymond.

'What do you suggest?' said Matthew. 'Get your hands off my chips.'

'Hang about,' said Alex, tottering, looking across the car park.

'Are my eyes deceiving me, or am I drunker than I think?'

Parked quietly, darkly beside the far wall was an army careers van, camouflaged with splodges of green and brown paint and covered with pictures of uniformed men gritting their teeth like Burt Lancaster, and tanks trundling over the debris of broken cities.

'Shit,' said Alex, incredulous, 'do they really think we'll sign on the dotted line?'

We stood there, in our identical apparel, each of us a reflection of the other in our parkas, scarves, jeans, and plimsolls. Matthew seemed to consider.

'You'll never get me to wear a uniform,' he said.

We all thought about it for a while.

'Hell,' said Alex, 'tomorrow's Saturday. Let's do something. Let's go camping'.

'Where, for Christsakes?' said Matthew, tossing his chip paper into the dustbin.

'The New Forest,' said Alex. 'Yeah. That's it. The New Forest. I can see it all like a vision.'

'You're seeing visions 'cos you're drunk,' said Raymond, wryly.

'Back to nature,' continued Alex. 'We'll live like the earliest man, living off the fruits of the land. Baked beans cooked by firelight. You gonna come?'

'It's near Southampton,' said Raymond.

'So what do we buy scooters for?' said Alex, slightly angry, 'to ride up and down the high street? To circulate around the car park until the end of time? When are we going to use the bloody things?'

The car park, the whole world seemed to be revolving crazily around me. I slid down the wall, turned and stretched myself heavily upon the cold ground, groaning, my lips almost kissing the dirty bricks. I just had to lie down. I could hear my friends' voices, growing unimportant and muffled by the whirling roar in my head.

'Hey. Just look at him.'

'Pick him up for Christ sake.'

'Shit. He'll be alright. Just leave him.'

'No doubt it'll be me,' spoke Alex's voice, 'dragging him all the way home tonight.'

I opened my eyes, vowing that never again would I drink with such abandon. Never again. For never before had I drunk so much. I closed my eyes and all the blackness in my head went swirling, rushing, heaving, up, skyward, tilting so far that I felt I might roll off the pavement. Rocking this way, then I went, it seemed, as though my brain were an overbalanced rocking chair about to topple over and crash, but no, not quite, then speeding giddily back to the opposite, furthermost peak of its absurd sickening momentum.

'Great. So we've finally decided to go camping,' spoke Alex, far away. 'So who's going to take me?'

I raised my lolling head from the wild, oscillating ground, felt the overwhelming sensation of drunkenness finally overpower me, felt my throat gagging, my stomach constricting and heaving, then I spat, once, twice, then threw up abundantly onto the pavement.

Chapter 5

Saturday morning, at precisely ten o'clock, found us speeding along an incredibly wide highway, our backpacks laden with sleeping bags and blankets, our helmets on our heads for once, and our eyes watering in the wind. Raymond suddenly shot past me, Alex riding pillion, asleep, his arms folded across his chest.

We kept at a steady fifty miles per hour. The sun blazed in the sky before us, huge and yellow, straining upon us with a blinding intensity. Raymond worked his way into the lead. His wasp-yellow SX 200 had been especially washed and his front-rack was packed with equipment he didn't really need; it just looked good.

Owen overtook me and screamed past Raymond before changing into top gear. Raymond changed down, opened up and overtook Owen. Matthew sped past me unexpectedly. I wrenched back my throttle and overtook Matthew and Owen. That's the way it went for ten miles or more.

We came to a Wimpy bar, set back in its own territory of tarmac and flower beds, and stopped for hamburgers and coffee. Our faces by then were streaked and dirty. We sat, slumped by the window watching the traffic. Alex hid a penny under a plate for a tip for the waitress, then back onto the highway we went, hurtling toward that hot high, unconquered sun and that forever distant horizon, irrevocably to the end of the world, it seemed.

When dusk had powdered the sky, and the moon could be seen like a pale galleon floating on the misty eddies above us, we had reached the New Forest. We rode several miles as though through a deep-green, and brown tunnel, opened to the sky. We turned off along a narrow, rutted track and continued our way into the very depths of the woods.

Owen, taking the lead, accelerated, nose lifting, back wheel spinning. He slowed, rocked once as though to stop, shot forward under a low-hanging branch, steered sharply around a large stone, picked up speed, and cut off swiftly to disappear. We followed. The trees enmeshed us, tall and blotting out the dimming light. We parked together in darkness, the intertwining branches above us like a canopy.

Raymond nudged Alex, as he had fallen asleep again, and he clambered off, blinking.

'We've arrived, then,' he said, suddenly shivering.

Raymond pulled his scooter up onto its stand, as Owen went off to find some wood to burn.

As night drew in around us, bringing with it the thickening darkness, filled with rustic smells and nocturnal noises, we had a fire safely burning and our baked beans steadily cooking. Alex, having forgotten to bring any eating implements started eating his with a screwdriver. Later I brought out my harmonica. Alex began singing in a gruff, mock-negroid voice.

'*Well, I woke up this morning...with an arrow in my back.*'

'Go on, Jack play something.'

'Yeah. Blues from Laurel Canyon. Y'know? John Mayall.'

'How about Blues from the New Forest?'

I played *Oh Susannah* instead, the only tune I could play. Owen built up the fire with twigs and its heat-giving flames danced and reflected on our faces. It was getting darker. The blackness of the night, beyond the fire, pressed in upon us. We wrapped ourselves in our blankets like Arabs in the desert. An owl hooted high

31

up in a tree, and something skipped from a branch above us.

'What was that?' yelped Alex, suddenly, his face completely concealed by his blanket.

'It was just an owl,' said Raymond.

'No. Before that.'

'I didn't hear anything.'

'You sure? I thought I heard something like a wolf howling.'

'There aren't any wolves in the New Forest.'

'Could have been a dog,' said Matthew.

'No. It was a wolf,' said Alex. 'There's a pack of them out there, lurking in the woods, and as soon as the fire goes out they're gonna slink in through the trees and tear us apart.'

'Great,' said Matthew, his teeth chattering.

The morning was glorious. I awoke with a start. The others were already up, huddled together, smoking. I rose, rubbing my eyes, feeling stiff and damp. Alex passed me a lighted cigarette. The forest was alive with woody, hectic smells and birds sang to us continuously. The sunlight sifted through the trees like bars of light and lit us in a lavish flowery haze. We loaded our scooters, then recommenced our journey, riding for endless miles, through continents of forest, centuries of beauty, through countryside that seemed to have no limit or boundary.

It was dawn and the sun yawned, so low in the early morning sky. Rabbits scarpered across the road like motivated balls of fluff, and deer, graceful and silent, bounded along among the trees. We revelled in all this limitless universe of unadulterated woodland, seemingly un-raped by the hands of man. Mile upon mile we travelled. I rode alongside Raymond, and Alex reached out to me. We shook hands. Through an eternity we sped down that misty-quiet, traffic-less stretch of road. The trunks of the trees blurred past us, ferns and flowers nodded at us in the heightening sunlight, basking in the beauty of that dappled wood.

Presently, after several miles, a large imposing, red-bricked hotel, like you'd expect to see on the seafront at Brighton, or Paignton, slowly rose from the horizon, as quiet as a whisper. Laid back in its own parkland of billiard-green grass, it stood, silent, grandiose, growing in size like a mushroom as we drew closer. We soon reached the private turning. The hotel stood grand and flashing with a thousand cleanly-lit windows; several flags, like on a seaside town promenade, flapped in a slight breeze, on tall white poles.

Unexpectedly, Raymond turned off and rode down the wide smooth road that led to the large, glass front door. Alex turned around and looked at us, puzzled, then laughed. We followed, mildly surprised. We all stopped haphazardly in front of the door.

'What did we come here for?' asked Matthew, looking around him.

'It's time for breakfast,' said Owen. 'Isn't it?'

Not far away on the lawn were white enamelled wrought iron tables and chairs interspersed with large striped sun umbrellas. A middle-aged couple sipping tea from delicate tea-cups eyed us disapprovingly. I looked up at the huge hotel entrance between two enormous stone pillars. From the darker interior of the place a doorman appeared, attired in a stiff, heavily-buttoned uniform. He was about fifty and looked a real humourless character. He stood on the steps, his hands behind his back, rising and falling rapidly on the balls of his feet.

'Move on you lot,' he said, almost sneering. 'We don't want the likes of you here.'

I was angered by his remark.

'We came to buy a meal,' I told him.

'You couldn't afford it,' he replied. 'Anyway, it's a private club.'

'What d'you mean *private club*?' said Raymond, getting hot under the collar. 'Where does it say *private club*?'

'Just piss off,' the doorman replied.

'Piss off yourself,' said Raymond bluntly.

The couple under the sun umbrella smirked at each other, obviously enjoying our tirade of insults.

'Aaarrhh,' said Owen sadly. 'Can't we have breakfast then, after all?'

'I'll give you one minute,' said the doorman, looking at his watch as though to time us. 'Then I'm going to phone the police.'

'You're gonna what?' I said, vaguely amused. 'We haven't bloody done anything.'

'I won't tell you again.'

'You stupid old fart.' I called him, wondering if he'd come down the steps and attempt to hit me. He didn't. He was quite unperturbed by my remark. He really got to me, though. Just because we rode scooters I suppose he thought we'd bust up the place. If it really was a private club he could have informed us politely. I couldn't stand rude shits like him.

'Are you going?' he asked impatiently, pretending to be counting the passing seconds on his watch.

'OK, OK,' said Alex.

Raymond sped away, straight across the vast lawn, just missing the tea-sipping couple by inches. They jerked back in their seats in horror. We followed, weaving patterns across the squelching, dew-wet grass. We gathered at the top of the drive.

'Stuck-up shits,' said Raymond, put out, blipping his throttle impatiently.

'It's "Joe's Cafe" for the likes of us, then,' I said.

'So it's "Joe's Cafe". If we can find one,' he replied, slamming into gear and speeding off. We followed after, wheels skidding and the breeze gusting into our faces, as though we might suddenly die of starvation if we flagged. Forever rushing, we were, it seemed, forever racing against each other and the impending Monday mornings and the night storms, the passing of time itself, as though our very youth might inexplicably evaporate from us, leaving nothing but wasted wrecks of our former selves. Such was the pace we maintained.

Chapter 6

One brittle January night it was so cold I almost cried. I rode through the frozen, quiet, deserted town, waited at the traffic lights for so long that I thought they, too, had frozen, turned the corner and slid, spinning, on an unexpected patch of black ice. I rolled into the kerb amidst a shower of sparks, cursing for my life, and my scooter ended up against a *no waiting* sign. I picked myself up, thankful that I was unharmed, lifted my scooter from its twisted position and heaved it upon its stand. I walked around it swearing under my breath. I straightened the handlebars as best I could, started up again, and hurried, wobbling rather badly, down to the Youth Club.

The place was life-savingly warm, and crowded. I joined my friends by the juke box and stood there red-faced and shivering. Matthew bought me a cup of tea and I sat in an armchair to drink it. My feet and fingers felt detached, amputated from the rest of my body; so senseless and cold. Gradually I thawed and the hot tea warmed my body. The feeling returned slowly to my fingers and my feet as though they were being pricked by a thousand tiny needles. I fumbled with a packet of cigarettes and somehow lit one. I inhaled deeply and almost choked. Alex came over and sat next to me.

'How's it going?' he asked.

'Just great,' I said. 'I just came off my bike and nearly killed myself.'

'Hey?' he exclaimed. 'When?'

'Just now.'

'What did ya do, for God's sake?'

'I hit some ice.'

'You alright?'

'I'll live, I said. 'At least I think I will.'

'Well I never,' said Alex blowing through his pursed lips. 'How's the bike?'

'It's OK. Steering column needs tightening, that's all. I'll get Raymond to do it. He likes doing that kind of thing.'

We sat in silence for a long while, watching Sarah Trueman by the wall, talking with her friends.

'Christ. She's beautiful,' said Alex, at last. 'And that's an understatement.'

'Did Gary do it? Knock her off, I mean? He was on about it the other day.'

'What do you think? He was with her last night.'

We watched her talking and laughing softly, pushing a friend away in response to a comment or joke. Then she took her can of Coke from a table, propped her slender, well-blessed body against the wall and began drinking, her short-haired head cocked backward, her large brown eyes closed. Her Levis were hip and leg-huggingly tight, faded and patched, with turn-ups above her soiled plimsolls. Girls like her are so perfect they're unreal, until you get to know them, I suppose. I have a disposition in that I don't get to know many girls, really, being so painfully shy and all, y'see.

Alex nudged me gently in the ribs and spoke quietly in my ear.

'Can you just imagine screwing her, then.'

I could.

D'you think she does?' I said.

'I bet she loves it.'

'You think so.'

'Yeah. Bloody sure.'

'I wonder if Gary's been near it yet.'

I'd often wished I had his confidence, good looks and clever rap. He was never short of a girl, it seemed. I wasn't jealous. Not really. It was just seeing Sarah Trueman there, so sexually nice, and imaging Gary getting really close and intimate with her. In bed, perhaps. That would be too much for me to handle. I still regarded girls as being some mystic, untouchable species. Alex pouted his lips.

'Dunno,'

'He'll try, though, won't he?'

Alex laughed, leaning back and stuffing his hands into his jean pockets.

'Yeah. Course he will. Wouldn't you?'

'Course,' I said.

Alex scratched his nose.

'She'd suck you in and blow you out in bubbles.'

We sat in silence again.

'Could I have a fag, Jack?' Alex asked, suddenly.

'Sure. Help yourself.'

'What are we gonna do, then?' he said

'Dunno.'

'Hey,' said Alex. 'Let's go and watch that film.'

'That army careers film. They're showing it in the end room.'

'Are they showing a film, then?' I said. I really didn't know.

'Yeah,' said Alex. 'Don't you read the notice board?'

'No. I missed…'

'Shall we see it then?'

'You must be joking.'

'No. Really. Just for a laugh, I mean.'

'Well, yeah, OK. When's it on?'

'It's probably on now. Come on.'

We walked across the crowded games room where people were playing table tennis and bouncing on trampolines. We reached a closed door with a notice hung on it reading:

A film will be shown in this room
from 8 to 9 o'clock,
presented by the Army.

'It's already on,' I said, looking at my watch.

'Are we going in?' Alex asked, his ear close to the door.

'Sure,' I said. 'Just walk in.'

The room was dark. On a screen by the opposite wall a splash of colour flickered and bulged with uniformed images and vast brown landscapes. A taped voice filled the room. We inadvertently caused a slight disturbance trying to find somewhere to sit, tripping over the legs of people and dark chairs. We found a place to sit down. The film failed to interest us.

'Yeah, yeah,' Alex said in a loud voice. 'Join the army, get supplied with a uniform and a pair of boots, get your hair cut, travel the world, meet interesting, foreign people, and then shoot them.'

We both laughed loudly at that. A dark head turned and grinned.

'C'mon,' said Alex. 'Let's piss off.'

We caused another slight disturbance finding our way out again. We closed the door behind us.

'That was boring,' said Alex, 'to put it mildly.'

'What are we going to do, then?'

'I'm fed up,' I said, sighing.

'Aren't we all?'

'Let's go for a drink.'

'Can't be fussed. I'm broke, anyway.'

'Let's go for a ride.'

'I'm short of petrol.'

'You can come on the back of me.'

'No,' said Alex. 'There's nowhere really interesting to…'

'Let's walk around town.'

It's too cold. Anyway, that's a drag.'

'So what are we..?'

'Hang about,' said Alex. 'It's time for the funnies.'

'What do you mean? What are you going to do?'

The key had been left in the film room door. Alex looked around, pressed his back against the door and turned the key behind him.

'When the film's over they won't be able to get out,' he said, smiling.

'They'll be stuck in there all night,' I said.

'Yep,' said Alex. 'That's right.'

We walked away.

'Say, that's really funny,' I said. 'Almost as good as the time during that disco, remember? When I pulled out the plug and all the equipment went off. Everyone thought a fuse had blown. The DJ went spare. Some people even went home, thinking it had broken down.'

'Yeah,' said Alex, suddenly bored again, 'We're both a couple of ravers aren't we?'

Part II

Mary

Chapter 7

My first summer job after leaving school was clearing tables and washing plates in the Café Majestic, an efficient, clean-bricked, self-service cafeteria on the fringe of the car park. My responsibilities involved pushing a trolley around a spacious, black and white lino-floored jungle of tables and chairs, picking up dirty crockery and cutlery, wiping tables clean with a damp cloth, then returning with the loaded trolley to the wash room where it was all washed and rinsed in a large, rattling, hissing machine that made me jump with its unexpected noises.

I worked hard at my task, my mind clouded with dreams and fantasies to obscure the boredom, the monotony relieved only when friends would come to see me, sit in a noisy lump by the windows, and spend the entire day drinking a cup of tea.

I was beginning to think I was more like a machine, lightly oiled and synchronised, than I was a person. When the last few customers of the day were scattered within the café interior, hunched over their empty cups, gazing vacantly through the large windows, playing with the ashtrays, I would pause with my trolley, or lean on my broom and wonder.

'Where am I going to end? What am I doing here? What's to become of me?'

I was destined to be a rock star, or a poet, I thought.

I was lost in these reveries frequently, until the manager, a slight, softly spoken man with greying hair and a pin-striped suit, would step quietly from his office, tap me on the shoulder, and tell me to lock the doors, hang up the *closed* signs, send those last few customers out into the world, sweep the floor and finish clearing up. And so it went on. For a flimsy, mind-wasted wage packet, I was slowly rotting away. Until one day I noticed Mary, who also worked there. She was sixteen, thin, frail, and because of some genetic jumbling, some hereditary conclusion of a long distant cross-breeding, was blessed with a dark skin. Slightly more than a perpetual suntan, with a springy profusion of dark, electric hair, she had the appearance of a sun-bleached Latino.

Mary's contribution to the running of the place was to slap pieces of ham and cheese into slices of bread and soft rolls, wrap them in cellophane and place them neatly on plastic trays to be displayed and sold at rip-off prices. She did it with an empty expression and clean, thin fingers, her body curved over the table. I was late for work one morning and took a short cut through the busy kitchen to avoid the manager, and there she was, weeping, sniffing and cursing over the solitary task, a long-bladed knife in her hand, her eyes tired and distant. Then, suddenly, there was a commotion. She threw her knife down on the table with a clang and hurled the bread and rolls against the wall, just missing me.

'Screw this fucking place,' she screamed.

I stood transfixed. A kitchen assistant in a starched-white overall came over and pushed me along.

'It's alright, lad, she's just having one of her turns. She'll be alright. Just move along, there.'

I looked back from the swinging door and saw her crumpled against the wall, her hands covering her face, her long body quivering with sobs.

I went quickly to the wash room and shucked off my parka. Tony, a freckled, nervous, curly-headed workmate looked around, pushing a tray of dirty crockery through the machine.

'You're late, he said, curtly.'

'Yeah. Sorry. Hey, who's that girl?'

'What girl?'

'The girl in the kitchen. You know, the dark-skinned one?'

He ran his hand through his tangled locks of hair.

'That's Mary Hawker. She's crazy...and shag-happy,' he rubbed dirt from his clean white overall and took a broom from the closet. 'I tell ya, she'd go out with anybody. She fancied me last week.'

He went out into the courtyard and started sweeping dust into the air. I followed after, waving the flying motes away from my face.

'Did you go out with her?'

He stopped sweeping, momentarily.

'Are you joking? I wouldn't go anywhere near it.'

I wonder why I haven't seen her before,' I said.

'She's been on holiday for the last three weeks,' said Tony, sweeping again, then stopping. 'If I were you I'd put your overalls on and get to work before the manager comes.'

I walked into the staff room armed with a broom, a dust-pan and a brush, to tidy up. In the doorway I froze. She was in there, alone, sat at the end of the long table, her head resting on her hands, her back long and arched, a cigarette held between slender fingers. Her eyes were moist, and tear-washed. She seemed to be trembling. Wordlessly I started sweeping around her, pushing chairs under the table with a scraping sound. She pulled on her cigarette, and breathed in deeply. I moved closer, sweeping, looking at the floor. She exhaled the smoke through her clenched teeth. I looked up and our eyes met.

'Hello,' I said.

'I'm in your way,' she said, standing.

44

'No. It's alright. Really.'

She went over to the armchair by the window, her nylon apron rustling, and sat down again, crossing her brown, slender legs. The sun appeared slowly from behind a scudding cloud and sunlight shot sharply into the room, striking her dazzling hair with a nimbus of light. I held my hand above my squinting eyes.

'You're name's Jack, isn't it,' she said.

'How did you know?'

'You ride a scooter.'

'That's right.'

The stabbing sunlight eased with another passing cloud and the room dimmed. I took my hand down from my eyes.

'I've seen you around town with your friends,' she said, drawing on her cigarette, holding the smoke deeply in her lungs, then exhaling. 'I've often wondered what it would be like to be a moddy-girl.'

At that moment a hefty, broad-shouldered lorry driver walked by the window carrying a large carton. He looked in, saw Mary, then stopped. He dumped the carton on the ground and tapped heavily on the glass. She looked surprised, turned her head, then smiled. He said something we couldn't quite hear and started laughing. Mary stood up, knelt on the armchair, and reached over to open the window, her skirt hitched up around her thighs. The driver's voice amplified as the window opened.

'...seen you for a long time.'

Mary giggled.

'How are you, Dave, you filthy sod.'

'Much better now, after seeing you, darling.'

I continued sweeping, watching and listening. The driver, with his open-shirted brambly chest, and pencil tucked behind his ear, put his work-calloused hand behind Mary's head and pulled her to him.

'Just give me a kiss and I'll be happy,' he said.

She gave him a cheeky peck on his unshaven bristled cheek.

'That's all you're getting,' she said.

He looked sad, then smiled, bent down and picked up the carton again, grunting.

'Take care of yourself, luv,' he said, then walked on.

Mary closed the window, twisted around to sit down, considered, then stood up and reached over the table to crush her cigarette out in an ashtray. The door opened quietly and the manager stepped in. I instantly started sweeping faster. Mary looked up at him with a bored expression.

'Come on Mary,' he said softly. 'You've had ample time to feel better now. Back to work, please. And Jack...'

I stopped and looked at him.

'We've just had a delivery of new cups arrive. I want you to finish here and give Tony a hand to unpack and wash them'.

'Yeah. Sure,' I said.

He walked away, leaving the door open. Mary swore between her teeth, then poked her tongue out at the doorway. She walked around the table, came so close that our bodies were touching, then suddenly pinched my waist with her fingers. I was taken aback with pain and surprise. She reached the doorway, looked back at me, smiled, then walked away.

The following day was hectically busy. Three of the staff were away with various ailments, and six coaches stopped unexpectedly, unloading hungry customers into the cafeteria. Even at four o'clock the queue along the self-service counter snaked out toward the door in an

46

everlasting, summer-heat haze. Tony and I worked ourselves into a sweat, circulating and clearing away the debris from the tables. Then a castor fell off my trolley, spilling plates onto the crowded floor with a shattering pandemonium. Everything seemed to be going wrong.

In the washer room the dirty crockery had accumulated into mountains, and then, with a sucking noise and a trembling rumble, the washer machine ground to a halt. The manager flustered up to me in his shirt-sleeves, rubbing his brow.

'Uh...Jack, you'd better take a break. You haven't stopped since you've been here. Take 40 pence worth of food from the counter. We'll try to get the machine mended, if not, I'm afraid you'll have to work late tonight because....'

He broke off in mid-sentence as a telephone rang, then walked briskly to his office, excusing himself politely past the clean-white attired cook who was carrying a tray of puddings.

I cursed at the thought of working late, but was relieved to have a break. I took a can of Coke and as an assortment of cakes and went into the staff room. Tony was sitting at the table reading a newspaper, his fingers poised to pick up his cup of tea. He looked up as I entered.

'All this bloody work.' I spat. 'I've got to work late tonight.'

'So have I,' he said, picking up the cup and sipping his tea. 'It's all overtime.'

'Shit. I wanna go out tonight. I feel I'm missing out on something if I'm forever working,' I said, biting angrily into a cake. I gazed through the window, calming down slightly, and saw a wasp hovering and zigzagging around a dustbin. I thought deeply.

'That Mary ....where does she live?'

Tony cracked his paper and looked at it intently.

'What?'

'Mary Hawker. Where does she live?'

Tony looked irritated and his left eyelid twitched.

'Why'd you keep asking questions about her for? D'you fancy her or something?'

I blushed

'...well, yeah. I think she's quite a character.'

He snorted.

'Why don't you ask her out then?'

I paused.

'She's in the kitchen,' said Tony, 'go and ask her out.'

'What do I say?'

He started reading his newspaper again. 'Dunno.'

I finished one cake and started another, pulled the lid from the Coke with a hiss, and started drinking it, thinking.

'Why don't you take her trays back?' said Tony.

'What trays?'

'The plastic trays she displays the rolls on. I washed the dirty ones before the machine broke down. You can take them back to the kitchen, then you can ask her.'

As I walked toward the kitchen, my heart hammered in my chest. Asking girls out wasn't one of the easiest things I could do. I nearly always blew it by saying something stupid. I was no smooth talker. I was full of hang-ups where girls were concerned. I could see her at her table through the open door, deep in thought, slowly cutting slices of cheese, her knife blade glinting. My guts were slowly melting into hot liquid. I felt like I wanted to go for a shit instead. Perhaps that's what I should have done, I thought, forgotten the whole idea. It was just a frightening ordeal. What was I going to say to her anyway, for God's sake? I could just imagine her face, looking at me in horror.

'What? Me go out with *you*?' she'd say.

She'd probably stab me with the knife she was using. And what about the other kitchen staff? When she'd snubbed me they'd all turn away and snigger, their hand over their mouths, thinking what a schmuck I was. Christ. My head was full of morbid visions. What I'd give for Gary's charisma and charm at that minute. No. I couldn't do it, I decided. It wasn't the time or place. I'd have to catch her at a disco or some such place one night, then I'd be drunk and confident and be able to talk like a smoothie and impress her with a load of bullshit. I'd return her trays, and that's all.

The kitchen was steamy and hot, bright, spacious and clean. The cook was rushing about, his tall white hat toppling about on his head, opening and closing cupboard doors, trying to find a bag of sugar. Saucepans bubbled and tinkled all around me. The cook brushed past me in exasperation.

'Can't find anything in this.... workhouse.'

He half-ran down the tile-chequered corridor to the store-room. I stood close to Mary and placed the trays on the table. She seemed not to notice me. The other staff must have been having their tea-break for we were now alone amidst all the smells of cooking food and the constant bubblings in the large saucepan.

'I've returned your trays,' I said.

She ignored me and cut a slice of cheese neatly in half. I watched her expecting some response. A tiny cloth cap was perched on her head, like a feather caught and stuck in black candy-floss. She blinked and turned to face me. The expression on her face was one of sadness and boredom, a sheer blank countenance telling of so many hours of repetitive, mindless motions, thinking, musing, making her rolls, wishing time away until the next tea-break, or five o'clock. She was, most probably, feeling the same way I did while pushing my trolley around the jungle, wondering what surprise the future might have in store for me around the corner. We both had that in common, at least.

She was looking at me and through me to the far wall at the same time, somehow. Perhaps I had become transparent. Being so close to her for the first time, though, she didn't seem as pretty as I first thought she was. It was her hair that sent me; that *frizzly* explosion of black electricity that crowned her head.

'I just wondered...' I said suddenly. 'Wondered...'

Go on. Go on. I nagged myself, ask her. Now's your big chance. There's no-one about. Do it. Go on. Do it.

'....if you'd like to...uh...come out...' I said, my trembling voice trailing way.

'Are you asking me out?' she asked, surprised.

'....uh. Yeah,' I finished with a final conviction.

So that was it. I'd done it. Now would come the looks of horror, I supposed. Now she was going to drop her knife and put her hands to her mouth and scream, or laugh, or whatever she was going to do. God. What had I done? She'd be telling her friends in the staff room, giggling over their tea cups. I was going to be a walking joke, if I wasn't one already. All the whispering voices would be about me now, without doubt. I shouldn't have asked her straight out cold like that. I should have gotten to know her better so that I could have gotten around her certain rejection in a jokey, 'never mind aye kind of way'. It was all a bit too dogmatic. I had gone about it all the wrong way. To my surprise, and relief, she looked pleased, and smiled, then continued working, cutting her cheese.

'I'll see you tonight,' she said.

'I have to work late,' I replied, stunned.

'Till when?'

'Till after all the washing-up's done.'

She seemed to consider briefly.

'I'll be down Cobham tonight. If you're around by ten you can take me home.'

The cook returned carrying a large bag of sugar. He dumped it on the table, looking at me.

'Come on, son, you can't stand there talking with all this work to do,' he said.

I made to walk away.

'I'll meet you at the bus shelter,' said Mary, looking down and cutting cheese again, 'Don't be late.'

The cook started stirring a large saucepan of soup, smiling to himself.

Chapter 8

Tony and I finished work at 9.30pm. Mary left, as usual, at five. The washer was not repaired and all the washing-up had to be done by hand. I felt tired, my hands red, sore and wrinkled. We walked around to the car park.

My scooter, parked by the crumbling wall, looked immaculate, smoothly-streamlined and laden, overloaded with chromium accessories. I had spent weeks repainting it, boundless hours washing, cleaning and polishing it, and now I was proud of my labours. The brash yellow rectangles of light from the still-lit cafeteria washed it in colour and cascaded it with sparkles. And when, finally the cafeteria lights were turned off, and we were plunged into the moonlight, the thing glowed in a dull, monochromatic haze, like a Chinese-puzzle of chromium bars.

Tony stood in the new darkness, buttoning up his overcoat.

'You did it, then.'

'Yep,' I said.

He tutted. 'She'll have your cock out in ten seconds.'

He started his moped, revving it screamingly, mounted, then disappeared into the night streets, home to bed and cocoa. I rode through the town, my headlamp boring into the semi-darkness, heading for the sea and a bus shelter, and a dark-skinned girl named Mary....

Cobham was our seaside resort, two miles from the town. Popular with holiday-makers, it was, however, a sleepily non-eventful place. A peacefully unpretentious huddling of fishing boats and tea-shacks. Its sparse attractions consisted of a harbour and a bar, a concrete promenade, a beach like a cobbled street, boat trips to the horizon and back, run by scruffily-dressed fishermen, and a fun-fair which travelled the country to return annually to pitch its tents on the mud of a nearby field.

That night it was busy with holiday crowds. I reached the bus shelter, stopped, and pulled my scooter up on to its stand. I could hear music from the fun-fair drifting on the warm air, and the sounds of colliding dodgem cars and girlish screams. The shelter was dark and empty. I sat on the hard wooden bench and waited.

People were milling and wandering past, looking redly sun-burnt and smelling of body heat and suntan lotion, still wearing tee-shirts and sun-hats. In the harbour, fishing boats bobbled about like fishing floats, rising and falling with slapping waves, squeaking. I lit a cigarette and inhaled deeply. A bald-headed man in a suit stopped opposite me and started shouting irritably at his immensely shapeless wife. I exhaled smoke from my lungs. They stood glaring at each other, then moved along again in a frozen silence. A young couple, dusty brown and shivering near-naked sauntered past them, carrying towels. I drew on my cigarette again, watching a scruffy black dog trot up to a nearby telegraph pole, lift a hind-leg and urinate, panting, its wild eyes darting all around.

Across a large patch of grass and flowers, the tea-shacks were brightly lit with coloured bulbs, emitting wafting, oniony smells. Small queues waited patiently. Some of my friends suddenly appeared, riding up to a tea-shack and stopping under a moth-blitzed street light, their scooters glittering. I waited a while longer, finished my cigarette, tossed it on to the ground and walked over to join them. Raymond was eating crisps, digging his fingers into the bag with a crackling sound. His eyes widened when he saw me.

'H'ya, Jack. Where have you been all night?'

Alex, a red beret on his head, stuffed a last piece of hamburger into his mouth and threw the paper over his shoulder, leant back on his backrest and folded his arms.

'How's it going?'

'I had to work late,' I said.

'That's a drag.'

Owen came over from, the tea-shack counter with a bar of chocolate.

'Hi,' he said, smiling 'D'you want a piece?'

'No thanks. What are you lot doing tonight?'

Alex sighed and scratched the back of his head.

'Nothin',' he said. 'Much.'

'Why? What are you doing?' asked Owen, breaking off a piece of chocolate and placing it in his mouth.

'What's anyone doing,' Alex laughed.

'Well,' I said, looking back at the empty bus shelter. 'I was supposed to be meet…'

I heard Mary's voice. We all looked around. The back door of a dirt-covered Ford Escort, parked darkly beyond the lights, suddenly burst open and her long brown legs kicked out. She pulled herself out, struggling to her feet, fumbling and pulling up her tights, sobbing. She slammed the door loudly, then ran over to me, wrapping her arms around my body, hugging me tightly, trembling, her crazily-dishevelled explosion of hair tickling my lips, her hips pressing hard against me. I was too surprised to speak. My friends stood and gaped.

'He almost raped me,' she said, her head on my chest, her voice thin and frightened.

'Who?' I said, amazed. I looked across at the car and it started up with a clank and sped away, its headlights blaring on as it disappeared around the corner. 'Who was it?'

'I didn't know his name,' she said still not looking up. 'Take me home, Jack. Please.'

Raymond screwed up his crisp packet and threw it on the ground, clicking his tongue. Alex was hiding his smiling face behind his hand.

'But what were you doing in there, anyway?' I asked, feeling angry.

A holiday maker walked from the tea-shack holding a hamburger in each hand.

'You should go to the police,' he said.

'She looks scared shitless,' said Owen.

A woman came over and looked quizzically.

'Is she alright?'

I looked at the woman, then down at Mary, as she sobbed and sniffed.

'Just take me home,' Mary said.

I rode carefully through the dark, slumbering streets, turned at the traffic lights, passing the black unlit shop windows, the mannequins in their static, frozen poses, and up the shadowed road. Her legs were gripping my side tightly, her arms loosely around my waist, hissing and whispering directions in my ear. We turned off up a long, bumpy hedged track and stopped outside a darkly lit bungalow.

'This is where I live,' she said. She pretended to fall off and giggled. 'Thanks for the lift.'

She got off and started walking up the front path.

'Hey. Hang on,' I called.

She stopped and turned to face me, standing in the moonlight.

'What do you want?'

I pulled my scooter up on to its stand and walked up to her.

'D'you feel alright?'

She looked at me, her face expressionless, her eyes like dull white lights.

'I feel fine.'

'Are you going to tell your parents?'

'About what?'

'About the guy in the car, of course.'

She looked bored.

'That was nothing. I'm used to it now.'

'Well, anyway,' I said, bemused. 'I was meant to see you tonight.'

'You're seeing me.'

'You know what I mean. I thought we had a date, or something like that.'

'You arranged to take me home, which is what you've just done. Thanks.'

I looked down at my plimsolls, then turned to walk away. She reached out and grabbed my waist, pulling me to her. I turned to face her and she pressed her hips against me again, smiling.

'You poor boy,' she said frowning, then smiling again. 'D'you want to give me a goodnight kiss?'

'I'd better just go,' I said, looking into her eyes.

She started rubbing her nose against mine, her lips opened, poised, breathing hotly on to my face. Then she suddenly fell backwards and my arms shot out and grabbed her thin, hard waist. She laughed softly and put her arms around my neck, our faces very close.

'That's better,' she said.

'I thought you were going to fall over,' I said, my hands on her hips.

'I was only playing.'

'You're full of surprises.'

She took her arms from around my neck and started playing with my parka zip, tugging it up and down.

'I really enjoyed that ride on your scooter,' she said softly, not looking at me.

'You did?'

'Can I come out with you again?'

'Do you want to?'

'Yes.'

'When?'

'Tomorrow night.'

'Won't I see you at work?'

'I'm taking the day off,' she said, looking up. 'But you can pick me up here when you've finished.'

'It might be late.'

'Doesn't matter. I'll wait for you.'

I pondered.

'Alright.'

She looked pleased.

'Do you want to kiss me now?'

I kissed her.

'You're seeing her again, then,' said Tony, running his hand through his matted mass of unkempt locks.

'Yep,' I said, leaning on an empty trolley in the middle of the washer room. 'Tonight, and I want to get out of this place early, if I can.'

I walked hurriedly into the cafeteria, pushing the trolley, to clear the tables. It was nearing closing time and the entrance doors were already bolted, the last customers served, and the lights dowsed so that the last few eaters and tea-sippers were conversing in muted tones, enveloped in a dim, yellow light. The washer machine had been repaired so it didn't take long to wash the last cutlery and crockery, then close the windows, sweep the floor, polish the tables, tell jokes, stack up trays, switch off the lights, and gaze out into the dimly-lit car park.

'You gonna stay for a Coke?' Tony asked, blowing through his teeth, leaning on his broom.

'Nope,' I said. 'Gotta go.'

He might have laughed, but I was already outside, punching my arms into my parka sleeves, starting my scooter, and riding off...gone.

'I thought I'd better tell you,' said Mary. 'It's only fair. I'm going out with someone else.'

I stopped beneath a tall, mighty tree.

'You're what?'

'It's nothing serious.'

'But who is he?'

'His name's Clive.'

'Do I know him?'

'I doubt it. He's a greaser.'

'He's a what?'

'I'll chuck him if you want me to.'

'Doesn't matter.'

I looked at the passing hedge as we continued walking down the shady lane leading from Mary's place, feeling rather apart from her now, and pointless.

'Do you like my perfume?' she asked, walking closer to me. 'It's my mother's. Really expensive. I took it from her bedroom. She'll do her nut when she finds out.'

'It's OK,' I said, smiling weakly.

'Come on, 'she said. 'Cheer up. I'll chuck him alright?'

'I said it doesn't matter.'

She took my hand and interlocked our fingers so that we seemed manacled together.

'I hoped you don't mind walking down to Cobham. It's just that I like to walk.'

'It's OK,' I said. 'But we could have been there by now on my scooter.'

I was feeling insignificant and shallow, walking with her like doom. I looked at her. Her feather-soft, profusive hair swept, pinned back with golden, butterfly-shaped hair-grips. Her eyelids had been carefully made-up with a light blue tint. She was wearing a tiny, tight leather-looking bomber jacket, and Levis, tight around her voluptuous hips. I thought she looked great; almost too good for me. She looked at me and smiled.

We walked along the pavement towards the town. For a while we walked in silence and I counted the paving stones and watched the passing cars. Then she squeezed my hand, pushing me onto the road with a playful rejection. We passed the gaping alleyways, the slow-changing, colour-combinating traffic lights, and walked through the town, passing the closing shops, excusing ourselves past the late, last-minute shoppers laden with shopping bags and weeping children. Workers from the building sites clumped past us with dirty overalls and empty thermos flasks, watching her coldly, and thin, freckled youths jittered past, shooting shy, hollow glances at her. She frowned, resting her head upon my shoulder, delicately. And I felt unsafe, wordless and proud, insecure, as though she was as smoke, held in my hand for just an instant, only to seep through my clenching fingers and disappear into nothing.

We decided to go into a small, late-closing coffee shop. We slid through, past the silent, swinging glass doors, pondered along the self-service trays of rolls and cakes, decided not to eat, then walked up to the silver coffee machine and asked for two coffees. The assistant regarded us with a smile, scratching her head with a finger nail. She clanged our money into the till. We walked over to a table by the window, carrying our coffees and sat down, Mary facing me. She pulled a packet of chewing gum from her jacket pocket and offered me a piece. At the same time, she pulled out a packet of cigarettes and a lighter from the other pocket and offered me a cigarette. I took one and put it to my lips. She leant over the table, wheeled the lighter alight and I lit up. She put the lighter to her own cigarette, sat back on her seat, lit up and inhaled deeply. Then she chewed her gum slowly, smiling at me, holding my legs between her feet.

'I'll tell you a joke,' she said.

I sipped my coffee.

'Go on then.'

She paused.

'What's the difference between a nun and a prostitute in a bath?'

I thought awhile.

'Dunno.'

'One's got a soul full of hope, and the other a hole full of soap.'

We both laughed.

Chapter 9

We reached Cobham and walked along the sea front, breathing the sea air and watching the waves, titanic and foaming, rolling onto the pebbly beach with a roaring thrust, then sucking back with a dragging of pebbles and seaweed. Seagulls screeched and chuckled above us, swooping and dipping, helter-skeltering upon the currents of the air. Holiday-makers jostled past us with their foreign odours and talk of distant cities. The large sun was slowly fusing into the horizon.

'Shall we go to the fun fair?' Mary asked, suddenly.

I heard the brash sound of ancient records and the collision of dodgem cars in their endless circulations, far away.

'Sure,' I said. 'Why not?'

We wandered around the coconut shies, and I won a box of chocolates for splattering the bull's-eyes with pellets on the rifle range. Mary pulled me towards the brightly lit dodgem car stadium. We walked up the wooden steps and sat on the brightly-painted barricade beneath a large speaker spitting and crackling loudly, playing some really funky Motown soul. We watched the dodgem cars buffing each other, flashing and sparking with sharp electrical charges. Then Mary gripped my hand tightly, staring rapt-eyed before her.

I followed Mary's gaze. Dappled by the multi-coloured lights, a broad-shouldered, unshaven youth, clad in a leather jacket, was sitting in a dodgem car, waiting for the thing to start. His knees were up near his chin, a cigarette held between his teeth, his hair long and flagged with dirt. I looked at Mary.

'What is it?'

She swore between her teeth, still staring.

'That's Clive, Shit. I didn't think he'd be here.'

'Clive?'

She looked at me. 'Clive. The guy I'm supposed to be going out with.'

I looked across at him again. I watched as he sat menacing and tough in the tiny dodgem car, bullying a young fair-worker to bring him his change, shouting at a friend to sit with him, swearing at some poor girl with a loud, obscene voice, causing her to run off into the night, cold and frightened.

'He's as tough as nuts, he is,' said Mary, still gripping my hand tightly. 'Treated me like shit. He's a real bastard.'

The dodgem cars jerked into motion, instantly biffing and buffing. I stood up, the music from the speaker funking and chunking and wuthering into my ears.

'C'mon,' I said. 'Let's go.'

I was scared shitless.

Seemingly from nowhere, Clive's dodgem car suddenly slammed against the low, wooden surround, stopping in front of us. He looked up at me, then Mary, then at me again, his hard eyes staring, coldly, hatefully, like a sadistic policeman. His sneering face was a mask of sheer ugliness, his enormous nose casting a shadow over one entire half of his visage. What ever did Mary see in this monstrous lout I thought wretchedly as I also tried to think of my next move. He was a living, walking, talking Punch, that violent, wooden, hunch-backed puppet who clubs his wife and crocodiles at the bigger sea-side resorts. We all remained frozen in a motionless tableau, as though time, and everything else, had hiccupped, stopped and been photographed for just that instant.

Then Mary began shouting, her body taut, standing up next to me.

'You'd better not start any trouble, Clive. We're through. You hear?'

I grabbed her arm hastily and pulled her along with me down the wooden, creaking steps. I heard a scuffle behind me and then, without warning, felt a mind-jarring blow on my back, like the kick of a horse, blasting me forward on to the hard, dry mud and tufts of yellow grass. I span around, scrambling on my knees, trembling. My eyes shot up through the red mist of pain and saw Clive, his teeth bared, his eyes flaring, and Mary, pushing, straining with all her might against his heaving chest, her thin arms outstretched, almost buckling with all the effort she was putting into it, shrieking.

'For God's sake. Just leave him alone, Clive, you stupid sod.'

He suddenly relaxed his pushing and she tumbled on to his chest, panting. She stood away from him instantly, looking small and dwarfed and helpless against his immense physique. A crowd had gathered around us. Clive pointed at me as I struggled slowly to my feet, my left arm rubbing my back, realising, miserably, that no-one was venturing to help me out of this distasteful predicament.

'What the hell are you doing with that...that little rat?'

'I'm going out with him,' Mary shouted, 'and there's nothing you can do about it. So just piss off and leave us alone.'

He looked stupefied, then pained.

'You're *what*? Since when?'

'That's none of your bloody business.'

He grabbed her arm roughly, shaking her like a puppet.

'You stupid little bitch.'

'Get your hands off her,' I bleated.

Without warning his boot shot suddenly outward, kicking me sharply on the leg, knocking me over sideways like a ten-pin. I gasped as I fell to the ground again, my leg exploding with pain, my mind reeling with wild pictures of me being torn apart, limb by limb, by this oversized moron.

'Shut your stinking mouth,' he screamed crazily.

I scrambled on to my knees, but couldn't stand. The pain was stabbing into my leg like a knife. He hurled Mary away from him and she staggered backward trying to keep her balance, but fell on to her backside with a yelp. Then he advanced towards me.

This was a sickening state of affairs. The crowd stood watching, as if we were a part of the attractions of the fair, like a troupe of jugglers or acrobats, watching, apathetic to my plight, expecting me to do something stupendous to win the day, no doubt, like rip away my shirt, like Clark Kent, to reveal a Superman costume beneath. There were no tricks up my sleeve to surprise anyone. I was no Superman. I was still trying to stand, holding onto my leg. Then to my almost hysterical relief a monster of a man with his immense pot-belly bursting through his opened shirt sprang from the crowd and grabbed my assailant around the neck with his powerful arm. They tumbled heavily to the ground, grappling and grunting, Clive's neck still held by the stranger's vice-like grip.

'You leave them alone, you hear?' the stranger growled. 'Or I'll break your neck.'

He appeared to me like some supreme terrestrial bouncer, travelling the land and kicking undesirable heavies and the bullies off the surface of the world. Clive's shouting was muffled, but he was submitting, his legs throwing dust into the air. Mary came up to me and began helping me up on to my feet.

'Are you alright?'

'Yeah. Sure.' I mumbled. 'Let's just go. Shall we?'

We walked up to the seafront again in silence. I was limping badly, unable to put too much weight on the kicked leg. The pain was slowly dissolving from my back, but I was feeling nervous and depressed, and without the presence of my friends, scared and alone. I supposed Mary was thinking what a weak, spineless coward I was. I could only blame genetics for not building me like Steve Reeves, for not giving me a supple, muscle-rippling body of an athlete, for being diminutive. I was a harmless pacifist by nature. Just because I rode a scooter and wore a parka didn't mean anything. I had nothing to prove, or disprove.

'He won't do anything again,' said Mary, clinging to my arm, as I limped along. 'I'll get my Dad after him. My Dad hates him. So do I now.'

'He'll get me again,' I said, feeling angry at her. 'And he's got friends. The bastard will get me somehow.'

'He's just a childish bully. My Dad can handle him.'

'And I've lost your chocolates, the ones I won at the fair,' I told her.

I looked at her and grinned, then grimaced as the pain shot up my leg again. She grabbed my arm tighter.

'It really doesn't matter,' she said.

We decided to go for a cup of coffee. The place was as large and spacious as the Café Majestic, where we both worked, but that night it was deserted. In the far corner, in the shadows, Gary and two girls were giggling over empty tea cups.

'Isn't he one of your friends?' asked Mary, as we stood in the doorway.

'Yeah,' I replied. I was surprised to see him there. 'I wonder what he's doing here?'

'He's got two girls. Greedy sod.'

'Yeah. He would. He's like that. Go and sit down somewhere. I'll go and get some drinks.'

She nodded then walked over and sat at the table with Gary and the giggling girls. I bought the coffees and returned, still limping. I looked at Gary and nodded, then sat next to Mary.

'What's this she's been telling us about you getting smashed by some greaser?' said Gary, pointing his thumb loosely in Mary's direction.

'She told you that?'

'You got kicked or something.'

'Clive's a real bastard,' said Mary, sipping her coffee.

'He got heavy,' I told Gary, stirring my coffee. 'When he saw me out with Mary. That's all. Gave me a dead leg. Some guy helped me out.'

He clicked his tongue and shot a cold look at Mary.

'You going out with her then, Jack?'

'Sure.'

'What...old shag-bag?'

I looked at him, then at Mary, then at him again.

'What d'you mean?'

He clicked his tongue and raised his eyebrows. One of the girls sniggered and buried her face in one of his loose parka sleeves. Mary leant over the table, stared at him and started rubbing her foot up and down his leg.

'Why do you have two girls?' she asked. 'Both at the same time?'

He looked mockingly into her staring eyes.

'They're twins,' he said. 'I haven't decided which one I like best.'

The two girls giggled again and grabbed each of his arms.

'I think you're bloody greedy,' said Mary, still staring, unblinking. 'Bloody greedy sod.'

One of the girls looked at her disapprovingly.

'Do you always swear like that? It isn't very lady-like, you know.'

Her twin sister laughed loudly and leant back on her chair, her hand still clinging loosely around Gary's arm.

'Look who's being the lady,' she said.

'At least I don't swear,' her sister retorted. 'Like that.'

'You shouldn't really be going out with that old shagger,' said Gary. 'Really. I tell ya, she's nothing but a street moppet...a slag.'

I looked at Mary, then at Gary, feeling perturbed.

'Come off it,' I said. 'You're coming on a bit strong, cool it, will ya?'

I took Mary's hand but she shook it free, still staring at Gary with soft, bewildering eyes.

'You'll soon learn, Jack,' he continued. 'She's just no good.'

The twins giggled again and one of them started playing with a teaspoon, causing it to bounce, dance and tinkle on the table top. Mary turned from me, span on her chair and shot a cold glance through the window in to the cold night.

'Bloody shit,' she spat.

'See what I mean?' said Gary, suddenly standing up, smiling, pulling the girls up with him. 'Gotta go. See ya. Mind what you do with...that.'

He looked down at Mary and the twins hung on to him, like two juicy sun-ripened grapes clinging to a green parka-ed vine.

'Oh, by the way,' he said, remembering. 'There's a disco tomorrow night at the Club. You going?'

'Yeah,' I replied.

'See ya, then.'

I watched them silently as they stumbled across the empty cafeteria; giggle and shout in the doorway, then fade into the night, noisily. Mary was swearing to herself softly, and sobbing.

'He wasn't very nice to you.' I said. 'I don't understand it. He's supposed to be a mate of mine.'

She looked at me with hurt, wet eyes, looking so vulnerable and childlike that I felt immensely sorry for her.

'He's good looking, isn't he?' she said. 'I used to fancy him once.'

'He couldn't have meant what he said just now.'

'Everyone treats me like shit,' she said.

I sipped my coffee.

'Don't say that.'

'Yeah. It's true what he said, I am a slag.'

'Mary. Don't say that.'

She looked at me, unperturbed and unemotional.

'I know what I've got it for. Anyone who wants it can have it'.

'What are you talking about?'

'I'm talking about screwing. What do you think?'

She leant sideways, dug into her jacket pocket and pulled out her cigarettes, taking one from the packet and putting it to her lips.

'Yeah. You want to screw me too that's why you're out with me.' She thumbed the lighter alight. 'It's alright. I'll let you.'

She looked at me, the cigarette held loosely between her lips, the lighter still in her hand, the flame gently spitting and popping.

'You won't have to rape me.'

She put the flame to her cigarette, drew on it, shut the lighter off with a click, inhaled, then blew smoke slowly through her pursed lips, an expectant expression on her face, returning the lighter to her pocket.

'Well?'

I put my hand on her arm.

'Look. I don't want to rape you. Or anything like that,' I paused. 'I'm with you because...because I like you.'

She ignored me, staring towards the far wall, unzipping her jacket, pulling it apart so that her young, well-developed breast beneath her blouse jutted and swelled with her breathing.

'Maybe you'll want it on the beach. Or on the cliff...' she turned her head to face me, a crazy look in her eyes. 'Or maybe right here, on the table.'

I was beginning to feel excited in an erotic, perverted way. Everything about her was getting uncontrollable, misty, insane. She lowered her eyes and giggled, her hair, a blizzard of curls, shivering.

She raised her head and drew on her cigarette. I studied her profile as she turned her head and blew the smoke slowly into the swirling air. My eyes followed the contours of her dark-skinned, warm scented body, sitting so close to me. At that instant the entire universe of sexuality seemed to have been grabbed, stuffed, crushed, vice-squeezed into her tight young frame. Her aura of lust and covetousness enveloped me with a tightening of the stomach. Even the cigarette she held in her slender fingers suddenly became a phallic object.

I felt a hand on my shoulder. I looked around, surprised. The cafeteria manager had walked over to us quietly and now he was looking down at me with a stern expression.

'We have in fact, closed,' he said. 'Would you mind leaving now?'

I looked across the darkened, empty cafeteria and saw an elderly woman in a blue apron sweeping the floor and a young boy picking up chairs and placing them upside down on the tables.

'Oh,' I said. 'Sorry. I didn't realise.'

Mary stood and stared at him.

'We were just going anyway,' she said, smiling strangely. 'We don't intend to stay in this bloody stinking hole much longer.'

He looked at me with a bored expression. I smiled weakly, shrugging my shoulders. He looked at Mary.

'There's no need to be so rude,' he said. 'You silly little girl.'

'I'm not so little,' she retorted. 'And I can prove it.'

He rested his hands on his hips, sighing heavily, a wary expression on his face.

'And just what do you mean by that?'

She smiled at him seductively. I took her arm.

'C'mon Mary. Let's just go, shall we?'

She shook her arm free and brushed past me. Then she seemed to shuffle up to him with her hands behind her back, as though she were a child about to receive punishment for some unspeakable crime. She bowed her head and lowered her eyes, grinning.

'Do you want to have me?' she said.

He looked stunned. I covered my face with my hands in exasperation.

'What ever do you mean?' he asked, though I knew he had an idea.

'You know,' she almost whispered, fluttering her eyelids playfully.

'Have me. Just imagine sliding it up a sixteen year old girl. That turn you on?'

'*God*,' he spat, grabbing her arm harshly, causing her to jolt. 'Just get *out*...'

He pulled her roughly to the door, kicked it open, and pushed her out, with quick, punching thrusts of his outstretched arms. He turned to face me, his face red and angry.

'...*Both* of you.'

We stood in the cold, colour-spangled night. She started crying, cursing through her teeth. I looked through the glass door of the cafeteria and saw the woman who was sweeping the floor, and the boy, both transfixed, like amazed waxen models, their mouths open.

'What made you do it?' I asked. 'You're crazy.'

She looked at me, her eyes red. She burst into tears, wrapping her arms around me tightly.

'I'm sorry,' she sobbed.

Chapter 10

It was warm on Mary's front porch. I stood on the doormat, rubbing my feet, my hands deep in my parka pockets. She opened the door. I stepped inside and she slammed the door behind me, shutting out the night air, and the large, swimming moon.

'Come on,' she said. 'The front room's in here.'

She opened the door and we both walked in. The room was warm, darkly curtained, and cosy. In one corner the television flickered and bulged with a loud monochromatic presence, irradiating the room with an ash-grey glimmer, making the corners bulge and recede with dull shadows. Mary's father, still attired in his building-site clothes, red chequered shirt and dusty jeans, was splayed sleepily upon an armchair by the modern electric fire set in the far wall. He lifted a hairy arm, limply, and shot a glance at his watch, then continued watching the television.

'It's gone eleven, Mary,' he said.

She closed the door quietly.

'This is Jack,' she said.

He looked up at me from across the room and nodded.

'Hello, Mr Hawker,' I said.

Under the large, curtained window, opposite the door, Mary's mother was sitting comfortably at one end of the settee, dressed in her pink dressing gown and slippers. Her wood-brown hair was long and carefully combed, covering her back. Beside her, an elderly woman sat sleeping, her wrinkled, white-haired head propped upon a hand. She was snoring, softly. Between them, a young girl aged about six lay across their laps, watching the television with wide, un-tired eyes.

'That's my mother,' said Mary, and I nodded to her. 'And that's Gran, and Emma, my little sister.'

Mary's mother drew her eyes from the television and smiled at me.

'Hullo, young Jack. Had a good time?'

'Yes,' I said, and I smiled at Mary. 'We walked to Cobham and back.'

'Have you seen Jennifer?' said Mr Hawker, still watching television. 'It's gone eleven o'clock and she's still not home. Any more late nights like this and there's going to be trouble.'

Emma stretched her arms. 'She's going out with a French boy,' she yawned.

'Well. I'll give her a thump when she comes in,' said Mrs Hawker. 'Less of the yap or you'll go to bed. It's way past your bed time.'

Emma wrinkled her nose and nuzzled her head upon her grandmother's rumbling stomach.

'She is, anyway,' she said.

'Take Jack out into the kitchen,' said Mrs Hawker. 'Go and make him a cup of coffee. I don't like being seen in my dressing gown.'

'Alright old shypots,' said Mary. 'Come on, Jack.'

'Send the dogs out here, then, if you're going to go in there,' said Mrs. Hawker, waving a limp forearm, pivoted by the elbow.

'Mind they don't eat you,' Emma cried, now watching the television again.

'What are they, wolves?' I said.

'Almost,' said Mary, and she opened the frosty-glass, kitchen door.

Two large, pointed-eared Alsatian dogs came suddenly padding, panting and sniffing up to me, wagging thick, strong tails and reeking of canine-breath and dog food.

73

Mr Hawker leant forward from his armchair.

'Down. Lie down. Good boys.'

The two enormous dogs curled around his legs, thumping the carpet with their tails and darting the room with wild, excited eyes.

I followed Mary into the kitchen. She closed the door behind us and clicked on the light.

'Coffee, or cocoa?' she asked.

'I'd rather have you,' I said, and I grabbed her tiny waist. She moved her hips towards me, and laughed dirtily, pushing me away.

'Not now. That comes later, you dirty boy.'

I heard a muted cry from within the front room.

'Make us a coffee, Mary, love,' called her mother.

She looked at me and grinned.

'Alright,' she called back. 'How many?'

There was a pause.

'Just three cups. Gran doesn't want one. She's still asleep.'

Mary frowned at me. 'Sit down, do. You make the place look untidy.'

I pulled off my parka and draped it on the back of a chair. The kitchen was large, sweet-smelling and clean. The floor was tiled, and across the room, a white-wood construction of shelves held potted plants, books, matchboxes, opened letters, newspapers and pencils.

'You've a nice place here,' I said pulling out a chair and sitting at the table.

She took off her jacket, threw it on to a chair, stood at the sink and filled the kettle.

'My Dad and one of his mates completely modernised it. You should have seen it before.'

'They certainly made a good job of it.'

She plugged in the kettle, then leant upon the sink facing me, her arms folded.

'Do you want anything to eat?'

'No. It's alright, thanks.'

'You can have beans on toast, if you want it.'

'No thanks. Really.'

'Sure, thanks.'

She took a copy of *Jackie* magazine from the shelf and pulled a chair up to me. She sat down and pressed her knees against me and thumbed through the pages, pondering at the pin-ups of rock stars, then looking intently at the problem page.

I gazed through the still-uncurtained window, saw the high grassy bank surrounding the back of the house, now dark and silvered with dew, heard a dog barking shrill and alone, somewhere in the distance, studied the ancient-shipwreck design of the wallpaper. This was Mary's kitchen, and there I was, warm and befriended, after only one day.

'Listen,' she said, taking my hand. 'I'll read you a problem.'

'OK,' I laughed.

She folded the magazine and slapped it on the table, leaning over it, her head resting on her hands.

"Dear Cathy and Claire,"' she read. "My boyfriend has left me after two whole months. I'd do anything to get him back. I love him so much and thought he loved me too. We made love several times. Now I feel so suicidal. What am I to do? I am fifteen. Signed Desperate."

'Well. What's the reply, then?' I asked.

'Just hold on,' she said, then reading. "Dear Desperate," it says, "I think you are very unlucky to be in such a situation as this, at the tender age of fifteen. Don't try to forget him, but look upon him as your first love. Do go out more and find new friends to help you find a new interest, and possibly a new boyfriend as

75

well!" She pushed the magazine away. 'Stupid bitch. Fancy getting all screwed up over some bloke.'

The kettle was gurgling and bubbling and she stood up and switched it off.

'Some girls do,' I said.

She bent down, her knees clicking, opened a cupboard door and brought out cups and saucers.

'I don't,' she replied.

I heard the front door slam, distantly, then a murmuring in the front room, the sniffing and thumping of dogs, Mr Hawker's voice stating the time, then finally, the kitchen door opened and Jennifer walked in, red-faced and flustered, as though she had been running. She closed the door behind her.

'Want a cup of coffee, Jen?' Mary asked, clinking the coffee cups on to the saucers. Jennifer stood there, blonde-haired, full-figured but plump and freckled.

'No thanks,' she said. 'Hell. You should have heard Dad moaning at me just now. He said I've got to stay in tomorrow. I can't help getting home late. I had to walk all the way from Cobham.'

'This is Jack,' said Mary, looking for the coffee jar. 'Jack, this is Jennifer, my other sister.'

Jennifer looked at me briefly. 'Hi.'

'Hullo,' I smiled.

She pulled out a chair and sat upon it, breathing out exhaustively. 'Hey, Mary. Guess what?' she said, suddenly.

'What?' said Mary, spooning coffee into the cups.

'I'm going out with Pierre, that French boy. I've been with him all day.'

'Lucky you.'

'What's he like, though? You've been out with him too, haven't you?'

'Why? Don't you know?' said Mary, pouring the water into the cups.

'I've only been with him today. Did he try anything with you?' said Jennifer and she realised, and looked at me. 'Oh!... sorry.'

'He gets a bit dirty-minded when he's drunk,' said Mary, pouring milk into a cup of hot coffee and placing it in front of me. 'One night especially, he had me on the back seat of his car pulling down my knickers in no time.'

Jennifer frowned and looked at me.

'Aye, shhh. Mary. Your boyfriend's here.'

'Jack doesn't mind, do you, Jack?' said Mary, looking at me, placing the remaining coffees on to a tray.

'Open the door, will you Jen?'

She stood up with a scraping of the chair, walked across the room, and opened the door. Mary went into the front room. Jennifer closed the door, sat back at the table, picked up the *Jackie* magazine and started thumbing through the pages.

'How long have you been going out with my sister?' she asked, not looking at me.

'Tonight was our first date,' I replied.

'What do you think of her?'

'She's alright.'

Mary came back in. I began sipping my coffee.

'You seen that picture of Steve McQueen in there?' asked Mary.

'Yes. Fantastic, isn't he?' said Jennifer, holding up the magazine and studying the double-paged pin-up with wide, unblinking eyes.

'Yep,' I said, joining in with their wistful adoration, 'He's a lovely hunk of male.'

Mary closed the door. Jennifer laughed.

'You two make a great pair. You're both a couple of nutcases.'

Mary stood by the sink again and lit a cigarette. I sipped my coffee quietly.

'I'm going to bed,' said Jennifer, standing up, throwing the magazine on to the table. 'Mind what you two get up to. Goodnight.'

She opened the kitchen door, poked her head into the front room. Shouted goodnight, closed the door again, walked across the kitchen, looked back at us and smiled, then went to her bedroom.

'At last,' I said, looking at Mary. 'We're alone.'

She gazed at the wall vacantly, pulling on her cigarette. I stood up and walked up to her. I put my arms around her. She turned her head, exhaled smoke from her lips, then looked at me.

'I'm a bit tired,' she said. 'Would you mind going after you've had your drink?'

'Uh. Sure,' I said, feeling suddenly put-down.

'It's nothing personal, Jack,' she said. 'I'm just not in the mood for that.'

'I was only going to kiss you.'

'That's what you say.'

I took my arms away and went to the table. 'What else could I do? In your kitchen, with your parents next door.' I picked up the cup and knocked back the dregs of coffee. 'I'll go, anyway.'

'I'll see you out, then,' she said and she walked towards the kitchen door.

I pulled on my parka.

'I've been having so many late nights, lately,' she said, opening the door.

We entered the warm, sleepy television-ruled room again, and Mrs Hawker looked up at us. 'Off already, Jack?'

78

'I'm feeling really tired,' Mary said, 'I'll see Jack out, then I'm going to bed.'

'Good night, then,' I said. 'Everyone'.

Back in the cool porch again I turned to face her. She closed the door quietly and I held her in my arms. She smiled at me, her skin almost black in the dim light, her eyes half-closed, pressing her body against me.

'When will I see you again?' I asked.

'I'll see you at work.'

It's my day off tomorrow. But are you coming to this disco?'

She stifled a yawn. 'What disco is this?'

'The one that Gary told us about. It's on tomorrow night.'

I felt her warm, snuggling, sleepy body within my arms. She raised her head, her eyes closed, pursing her lips. I kissed her. She pulled away slowly.

'No,' she said sleepily. 'I'm staying in tomorrow night.'

'But it's Friday tomorrow, the weekend, and all that.'

She shrugged her shoulders, resting her head on my shoulder. 'So when will I see you again?' I asked, her hair tickling my lips.

'I'll see you at work,' she replied. 'I can't see you before that, I've loads of jobs to do around here. I'll be too busy.'

'That's OK,' I said, looking across at a picture on the wall.

'Goodnight, then,' she said, pursing her lips, looking up at me.

I kissed her. I stood beside my scooter, illuminated dimly in the moonlight. I gazed back at the bungalow.

Mary stood, etched upon the bright rectangle of the doorway.

'Be good, and don't flirt,' she whispered across to me.

She went inside and closed the door. I rode home slowly, thinking. I climbed into bed feeling tired and ready for sleep, but the bed was hot and uncomfortable and I couldn't relax that night.

Part III

Alex

Chapter 10

I was spread across Alex's bed, leafing through his *Scooter World* magazine and smoking a cigarette. He was brushing his hair in front of the mirror and scrutinising himself, regarding his reflection with nonchalant approval. He leaned back and flicked over the bushy quiff over his crown with the palms of his hands and posed with a flamboyant air.

'I couldn't have a drag, could I, Jack?'

I passed the cigarette to him and he sucked upon it, like he hadn't smoked for a week, and passed it back, hot and tasteless, devoid of constituency and flavour. He had smoked it dry with one drag.

'Thanks,' he said. 'Now, which tie will go with this shirt? Let's see now...'

He walked across the bedroom to his older brother's wardrobe and opened the door, peered into the dark interior and pulled out a large, black and white, striped tie.

'Perfect,' he nodded. 'He won't even know I've got it. He won't even know it's gone.'

He looped it around his neck, wound it into a really enormous knot and pulled it up tight.

'There,' he said.

He stepped back and regarded his reflection in the mirror with a frown.

'I don't know, though.'

'It looks alright,' I told him, knowing that if I wasn't sycophantic we'd be there all night. 'It looks great.'

'No. It won't do,' Alex said, and he pulled the tie from his neck and threw it on to his brother's bed. 'How about a white one?'

He went over to the wardrobe again and rummaged through his brother's shirts and trousers and pulled out another large, wide white tie.

'It's really a bore,' he said, 'knowing what to wear to look smart. Do you ever find that?'

'Sure,' I replied. 'It must be the same with everybody.'

'I don't know so much. Who else would take over two hours to decide which tie to wear?'

He ran his fingers over the tie he had selected.

'Let's think. A white tie with a blue shirt, and grey trousers. What do you think, Jack, O great one, O connoisseur of all fashionable things?'

'Yeah,' I said, 'it'll look alright.'

He tied it around his neck, knitted it and wound it, pulled it into another really enormous knot and tightened it around his neck.

'There,' he said, almost proudly, 'one large white tie is finally around Alex's neck. The streets will be thronged with rejoicing, and wine will fill many golden goblets, and the people will be fed and satisfied with the roasted lamb and fatted calf...'

'I don't know, though, Alex,' I said, studying his attire closely, feeling somehow that it wasn't quite right. 'On second thoughts. Do you think a white tie really goes with a blue shirt? It looks a bit...loud, yeah?'

'Perhaps you're right,' he mused, frowning at his refection. 'Yes. You're right. A white tie will not go with a blue shirt. It makes me look like Al Capone.'

He looked sad.

'What am I going to do? We'll be here all night.'

'What's the need for all this ultra-smoothness?' I said looking at the clock. It was getting late and I had to get drunk yet. 'We're only going to the Youth Club disco. You can wear anything. How about not wearing a tie, then perhaps we can get to the pub before they close.'

He stood transfixed, his countenance rapt with a mock-disgust, like some old man suddenly finding a dog stool stuck on the tip of his walking stick.

'Not wear a tie?' he breathed, aghast. 'Goodness gracious...'

'Who's gonna notice, anyway?' I said, 'whether you wear one or not,' knowing all the time who would....

Vanessa wasn't exactly Alex's girlfriend, but he was going out with her, sort of, but only when *she* felt she wanted to. It seemed to me that every time he saw her he was drunk, filled to the brim with superficial confidence, to rap and woo and win her over with wise or silly talk. She was always so cool, so nice, never unkind, but so pretty-pretty. I think she liked him, but not that much. I suppose you could say she was using him, or taking advantage...I really hadn't any idea what was really going down. Alex liked to give the impression that she was crazy about him. I knew she wasn't. I don't know. It was all a crazy game.

Every time they met, the encounter, to Alex was some nightmarish nerve-wracking ordeal. He felt he had to impress her endlessly with every movement made and every word uttered. It's a wonder his mask never cracked under all the make-up. Vanessa had him sussed, I reckon. Anyway, she was weary of his plans and deception; she had had time to learn. She first went out with him while he was still at Art College and he used to travel over fifty miles every night just to see her. On one impulsive spree he spent his entire year's government grant on a ring, just to express his devotion, almost starving in the process. It was the biggest expenditure of his life and she wore it for only a week.

Their romance had been a brief affair, an escapade into story-book mists, kisses at the front door, and coffees in the kitchen. He was so sincerely infatuated, and she so wide-eyed but unimpressed, what they were going through now was the tail-end of the affair, verging on the platonic to Vanessa's mind (I guess) though Alex couldn't see that. She was a soft, perfumed, growing rose, but a young flower blooming and withering in a tired sun. She was already planning to move away, live in the city and become cosmopolitan. She didn't need to love someone who spent his time treading the pavements of a small town, sleeping on windy beaches, drinking, dancing, building misty empires of nostalgic thoughts and forever painting portraits of her face, someone with eyes sometimes so sadly moist and withdrawn...

'Hello Vanessa,' he said going into a reverie, 'can I take you somewhere nice on my scooter, then perhaps take you for a quiet little drink? Well, just a teeny-weeny one, an orange juice, a Coke...a glass of water...please?'

He made a pitiful, mournful whimper, an amusing imitation of some poor soul really heartbroken and suffering in the throes of love. We both laughed at that. Then he ran across the room, plucked a large pillow from the bed and started kicking and thumping it around the room, scattering feathers around the place like a blizzard of snow flakes.

'So Vanessa Holmes. You don't want me then, huh?'

He kicked the pillow up to the ceiling and it fell to the floor again with a thud.

'Take that, and that, and that,' he shrieked and he kicked it and stamped on it, alright, had enough?'

I was rolling on the bed with laughter. Alex pulled off his tie and glanced in the mirror again.

'I wonder if God looks down at us?' he mused, 'or takes notes on our behaviour?'

'Well,' he continued in a God-like, deep, rasping, resonating voice, '*what shall I confront them with today? What emotional hang-up shall I give them next?*'

He scratched a long white imaginary beard in contemplation. '

'*Ah. I know. I'll give Vanessa to Alex, and possibly...um...let's see now, yes, and Mary, whatever her name is...*'

'Hawker.'

'Yeah.'

'*I'll give Mary Hawker to that poor screwed-up kid Jack. I bet he can't handle that one.*'

'You could imagine it though, couldn't you? God up there looking down at us...'

'*Yeah, tomorrow I think I'll give them both a puncture in the pouring rain, that should stump them.*'

We both laughed then he cracked his tie like a whip.

'What about this mother of a tie? I still haven't decided.'

'Look, I told ya. Don't wear one.'

'I've got to.'

'Well. Wear a black one then.'

He suddenly stood static, quite still with a grave expression on his face. He dropped the tie to the floor and stepped over to me and placed his hand across my forehead.

'You feeling alright? O-one of wisdom, O-distinguished designer of trendy garments, O-Mary Quant.'

'What's wrong with a black tie?' I asked. 'It'll look OK with that blue shirt.'

'I don't have a black tie,' he replied with a vacant expression.

'Shhiiit,' I exhaled in exasperation. 'Wear a different shirt then, if none of your ties go with that shirt.'

'I never thought of that.'

'Well, then.'

He went to his drawers and sorted through his socks and jumpers.

'Let's see now,' he mumbled, sorting through articles in the drawer, 'perhaps a pink shirt, or maybe...yes? I have it...'

He suddenly produced a shirt as though pulling a magical rabbit from a magician's hat.

'....a yellow one.'

He held up the freshly washed and ironed, yellow Ben Sherman, and smiled weakly.

'What would I do without your brains?'

'Never get time to enjoy yourself,' I replied, frowning.

He unbuttoned his blue shirt and pulled it off. He threw it on the carpeted floor and stretched his long arms, slid his hands into the sleeves of the yellow one, pulled and tugged his arms, pulled the shirt over him, and started to button it up. He stood tall and gangling in front of the mirror.

'Now then,' he breathed, 'which tie shall I wear..?'

Alex and I rode our scooters up the shop-window-illuminated high street and turned off down a one-way street. The town was quite deserted for a Friday night. I suppose everyone was either in the pubs, or at home watching television. Come to think of it, where else would they be? A young couple walked briskly along the dark pavement, swinging their linked hands together as they went, obviously in a hurry to get somewhere. We reached the Nine Stars, our pub, and parked outside, beside other scooters already there. The Nine Stars was a typical back-street pub, where the proprietors ignored the fact that we were all too young to drink. I bet that if it wasn't for our custom the place would have gone bust in a matter of weeks. I could see the jostling silhouettes of my friends through the thin red curtains. They would all be there tonight; it was expected, obvious, regular, and mechanical. After all, wasn't it Friday night?

When I opened the lounge bar door we met with an almost solid mass of people. Everyone seemed to be there that night, the gang, their parkas, great-coats and scarves hung upon the hooks on the door, their faces cleaned, scrubbed, shaven and patted gently with a light sprinkling of aftershave, nearly all wearing a large knotted tie and trousers slightly flared and freshly pressed. We were greeted with genuine acclaim, the sincere joy of friends who were pleased to see us. We closed the door, took off our scruffy parkas and hung them up.

Gary, Matthew, Owen, some others, and two girls I hadn't seen before were sitting around the table by the window, smoking, telling ribald jokes and bursting into gusts of laughter. Raymond was standing at the far end of the bar, listening and smiling. Yes, the place was actually full of friends who knew me, who might confide their most intimate problems, who might lend me money or buy me a drink. It was a good feeling. There were so many of us that night that the other local boozers, the fifty year old cider-heads with their red noses and gabardine raincoats, had been forced away by our number, and noise. Alex put his arm around me and steered me over to the bar.

'I'll buy you a drink,' he said.

Raymond nodded at us when we reached him.

'You're both looking smart,' he said.

Alex ran his fingers through his hair in his habitual manner.

'Smooth's the word, son.'

'I'll have a pint of bitter, Alex,' I said, smiling, thinking how long it had taken him to get ready.

'They've a good light show tonight,' Raymond told us as he sipped his beer, and a go-go dancer.'

'Hey. Wow,' I exclaimed, opening my eyes wide. 'That I must see.'

'She's ugly, Jack,' Raymond told me.

'Aaaarrrhhh. Don't disappoint him,' said Alex digging into his rattling pocket and raising a finger to attract the barman's attention.

'An ugly go-go dancer. Whatever next?'

'I've never seen one before,' I told them.

'What. An ugly go-go dancer? Raymond asked.

'A pint of bitter, and a Southern Comfort please, John,' Alex called to the barman while leaning toward the bar.

'No. A go-go dancer. Any go-go dancer.'

'Tonight's gonna be your big night, then,' said Raymond.

'What do they do, though, these go-go dancers?' I asked.

'They shake their boobs and thrust their crotches at you,' Alex told me, suddenly noticing the two girls sitting by the window with Gary, Matthew and Owen.

'Yeah?' I said in amazement. I enjoyed giving everyone the impression I was a bit thick.

John, the barman, handed Alex his Southern Comfort. 'You lads are all going to this disco of yours, I take it,' he said.

I nodded.

'Never had "go-go dancers" in my day,' he told me while pulling my pint. 'All we had was good music, and I mean good music.'

We liked John. He was a good barman, but being over fifty, and going bald, he couldn't understand what we saw in "dancing" to loud soul music. Glen Miller was, and always would be, the "greatest" in his opinion. He had a cassette tape recorder hidden under the bar and every record he ever made, recorded on tape. On quiet evenings he tried to educate our minds by playing the tapes, rather loudly, so that we couldn't talk easily without shouting and had to either go out or sit there and listen, with glum expressions on our faces. Mind you, I quite enjoyed *Moonlight Serenade.* One night when I was drunk, I imagined I was waltzing in slow motion a foot-deep in dreamy mists with Ginger Rogers or someone. I couldn't imagine John waltzing, though, even as a young eighteen-year-old. Seeing him now as a man, short, squat, and balding, it would be difficult to imagine him any other way. He handed me my pint and Alex paid him with his niggard coins. John counted them briefly, clenched them in his fist then went to serve someone.

'Cheers, Alex,' I said, sipping my drink.

'Who are the chicks by the window?' he asked Raymond, quietly.

I looked over and noticed one of the girls looking him up and down, giving him, not quite a look of admiration, or attraction, even, more a "I wonder what he's like in bed" kind of look, I guess. Girls never looked at *me* like that. But then, I wasn't as good-looking as he was, or as tall. That's the sort of qualities girls go for, isn't it?

'Owen and Matthew picked them up tonight,' Raymond told him, 'there's a whole crowd of chicks from Weybridge up there.'

'Up where?' I asked. I wasn't being thick; I just didn't know what he was on about.

'Up the disco.'

'You mean you've already been up there?'

'Yeah. Sure. What's the big deal?'

'I mean you're back here again.'

'So I am,' he said, pretending to realise where he was, then laughing.

I wish I could just walk into a disco without having to get drunk first. But then Raymond was full of real confidence.

'It wasn't very good earlier, Jack,' he explained, 'so I popped down here for a few more drinks until more people arrive.'

'Ah,' I said, sucking in my cheeks, as though that was the most logical explanation to such a stupid question.

'You mean the place is going to be full of women?' Alex asked, sounding quite happy, not expecting a reply. He smiled at the girl looking at him and she smiled back shyly and looked away quickly. He swallowed his Southern Comfort and turned to the bar to order another. He really confused and maddened me sometimes. He could get off with any girl he fancied, I reckoned, but again tonight, he'll be chasing Vanessa and she'll be using and abusing him as always. It was as though they had both their parts in the relationship written down like scripts and were both very bad actors. If he did go off with anyone tonight it would just to get Vanessa jealous. That's his style. If I were him I'd be screwing every girl in sight...

After my third pint I began to feel quite inebriated, and very happy. That's the way it affected me. Sometimes it made me depressed, but most of the time it was like this; a feeling that nothing could go wrong, that I could go to the disco and dance forever, that I could do something really crazy, just let all the energy burst out of me, just scream with the exhilaration of being young and full of life. I even felt I could walk up to one of the girls by the window, sit down right next to her and chat her up with a load of fancy-talking bull-shit and impress her so much that she'd think I was the smoothest-talking cat on earth. I started to realise lots of different things. I looked at John, busy behind the bar, and I felt as though I'd never seen him before. I marvelled at his shining, balding head and how incredibly old he was...I mean old old. Christ. What a boring old fart. I hope I die before I get that old. I'd never want to be as old as he was. A sudden loud roar of laughter filled the place and I looked across at the crowd by the window. Someone must have said something really funny because they were rolling about on their chairs, choking and laughing, teary-eyed. I thought I'd go and join them, but at the same time felt all excited and impatient. Alex and Raymond were talking about something so I interrupted them.

'Hey. Isn't it time we were getting to the dance? I mean we don't want to stay here all night...'

Alex looked at me and his eyes were sleepy and red. He was probably just as drunk as I was and he looked at me as though he was really looking around me. That's the way the drink affected him. He put his long arm around me to pull me in closer to confide some great magic secret.

'Tonight's gonna be the night,' he told me in a hushed voice, 'I'm gonna get Vanessa.' It was nice that

92

he always told me what was going on in his head, but tonight because he was intoxicated I found the situation very amusing. I could imagine him prancing, gambolling and bleating like some absurd ballet dancer, spinning a pirouette on his toes with an enormous net in his hands. I looked at Raymond and we both laughed. Alex was only slightly perturbed by our derision. He downed his southern comfort with a gulp.

'Yeah. OK,' he said. 'I'll get another drink, then we'll go. OK?'

I had a double vodka and lime which made me pull a few faces and see the walls throb. I started thinking about things again. I looked at Raymond's tie and was astonished at the size of the knot. He looked really smart. He must have taken ages getting ready, but I was pretty well dressed myself. I thought of all the millions of young people just like me, dressed up in their best threads for a Friday night. Then I thought of all the people who were as drunk as I was at that very moment. There must be millions of us scattered all over the surface of the earth, all in our private little worlds, all revelling in our own drunken imagery. Looking around at the faces in the bar I realised that every one of us was totally pissed, all drinking our chosen elixir of this universal, legal high, all smiling or laughing. It sure was a "happiness drug", I perceived. Alex suddenly banged his empty glass on the bar and it gyrated there briefly like a toppling spinning-top.

'Let's go then, shall we?' he said 'You coming with us, Raymond?'

He downed his beer quickly, 'Yeah. Hang on.'

We put our parkas on and stepped out into the rather chilly evening air. The three of us walked up the dimly-lit street. The rest would follow later. The Youth Club wasn't far so we left our scooters outside the pub. We could already hear the disco music being carried on the breeze; the Four Tops singing *I'll Turn to Stone*.

'Hey. Wow,' said Alex dancing lightly on the balls of his feet and spinning slowly around, his hands deep in his parka pockets. 'They're playing Motown.'

Raymond started singing, coughed, then carried on singing again...*take your love away...I'll turn to stone...turn to...*'

He appeared to me as a walking mass of tinkles. The front of his parka was almost completely covered with badges he had bought in the summer at a kiosk at Cobham. They were all bright and different colours, all over-lapping like the scales of a fish glittering under the street lights, and had thoughtful little statements on them that read "I like it" and "kiss me".

We reached the Youth Club car park. It was full of cars and scooters. The music sounded really loud from here. It was a wonder all the inhabitants of the nearby houses hadn't complained. Come to think of it, though, I expect they already had. But those boring old farts could go to hell. Our music was playing loud to show to the world we were young and having fun. Alex stopped and lit a cigarette, the brief orange flame of the match lighting up his cold, red face. He looked strangely tense and nervous and his hands were shaking, possibly with the cold, or more likely, with the thought of finding Vanessa in the disco, probably dancing with someone else.

We walked briskly across the car park, weaving around parked cars. I, too, was beginning to feel an excited sensation in the pit of my stomach. We were going to the Youth Club as we did almost every night, but this time it was different. Tonight we would have to make a big impression when we walked through the doors. We would have to look really cool, like we were some kind of super-studs. The place would be full of girls just waiting to be asked to dance. I was drunk enough to handle it. The music was growing louder and I could see flashing coloured lights through the large black curtains covering the window. We reached the porch. Just outside the doors a couple were kissing, oblivious to our presence. Alex suddenly grabbed my arm, stopped, then pushed both his hands deep into his pockets, his cigarette held loosely between his lips, blinking as the smoke went into his eyes.

'Shit,' he said. 'It's fifty pence to get in.'

I saw the notice beside the doors reading *Entrance...50p*, written in chalk on a small blackboard.

'So?' I said, knowing what was to come.

'I haven't got it, man. Look.' He pulled a few pennies from his pocket and held them out in the palm of his hand so we could all see them.

'That's all I've got...' he continued briefly. 'Twenty two pee...and a half...'

I tutted. He grabbed my arm and giggled, swaying slightly in the cold light.

'I'll pay you back, Jack, promise.'

'Come on. It's cold,' said Raymond. 'Let's get in there.'

'Yeah. OK. I'll pay for you Alex,' I said and opened the doors.

The place was quite crowded, smoky and hot with knots of darkened, dancing figures bobbing and gesticulating among those standing and talking. The music was loud and thumping, filling our ears. I had to shout to the man with the tickets when he asked how many I was paying for. We went through to the cloakroom to take our parkas off. Alex went into the loo to urinate as I flicked a hand over my hair, looking in the mirror.

'If she's in there,' he called over to me, 'with some guy, I'll bloody kill him.'

I knew he wouldn't.

'I don't expect she is,' I told him.

He came out, zipping up his trousers.

'Where's Raymond?'

The music was loud even in the cloakroom. I really felt like dancing.

'Dunno. I expect he's already on the dance floor,'

I began jumping up and down in time to the music. 'Let's get in there shall we?'

We went out and stood by the wall, our hands in our trouser pockets. The dark hall was suddenly filled with a riot of colour and the DJ mumbled something I couldn't understand into the microphone, something that sounded like "have a good time, ya hear?" The entire dancing city went wild when he played *This Old Heart of Mine*.

I looked around me. The large windows of the hall had been blacked over with large moth-eaten blankets, so that the place was lit solely by the coloured bulbs around the DJ's playing deck. It was hard to imagine this was the same hall we played table tennis, making a lazy sound of di-dock, di-dock. A platform had been erected near the DJ's equipment surrounded by spot-lamps. That was for the go-go girl to dance on, I presumed. A small group of girls stood near me. They weren't local because I didn't know them. One produced a packet of chewing gum and handed it around. Then she put some gum in her mouth and began chewing, her jaw moving slowly, her hips swaying with the music. A tall youth, in a really sharp suit, stood leaning against the wall, watching them, unsmiling. I began to regret Mary not coming out tonight. I just couldn't understand her staying in when

96

all this was going on. She was the sort of girl who did what she wanted, after all. I found myself missing her. I could have shown her what great fun I was to be with and danced with her all night. Still. I wasn't going to be sad.

Alex suddenly grabbed my arm and shouted into my ear.

'Look. I'll see ya later on, OK?'

He walked away and disappeared into the crowd like a fly in a fog. He had obviously seen Vanessa and off he had gone, to make conversation, to play his part in their weird game, to be rebuffed again in his eternal battle to win her heart. I craned my neck, trying to see where he had gone, but he was lost in the crowd. I stood awhile wondering what to do next. I thought I'd go and find some friends or go out to the Club bar and buy a Coke. I was feeling quite thirsty again. I looked over at the group of girls. They were still there, talking and giggling together. I wondered why nobody had asked them to dance yet. Then I told myself that I would do it. Yes. I would just walk over and ask one of them to dance with me. Being so drunk had made me feel brave. Yes. I would do it.

The DJ's loud, omnipresent voice moaned from the speakers as though he knew what was going on in my head. 'Yeeeeaaah. Keep on doing ya thing....' the music stopped momentarily, '....it's Isaac Haaaaayes..'

The guitar intro to the *Shaft* theme started playing, going *"chagga chagga whagga chagga"* and I cursed the DJ for his choice of record at that particular moment. It wasn't the easiest record to dance to, but I was resolved to get on the dance floor. I made to step over. If they had been local girls it would have been easy. They would have known me and realised that all I wanted to do was dance...all platonic and no hassle.

These girls would probably assume I was after their bodies or something. Shit. Why was everything such a bloody ordeal? I finally walked over and tapped the first girl I came to on the shoulder. Her face was expressionless when she turned to face me. Her friends stood very still, just staring at me. I guess I must have burst rather abruptly into their girly conversation. I shouted into the girl's ear, smelling her perfume, saying the first thing I could think of.

'...uh...wanna dance...?'

Her face was still expressionless. Then her eyes shot into me coldly as she shook her head from side to side, mouthing the word no. She turned to her friends again and they continued talking, as though the little incident never happened. It was like a heavy metal door gone "kerklash" right in my face. The music suddenly seemed very loud.

I walked back to my place by the wall. A verse of the *Shaft* record stabbed into me with a sardonic irony. Isaac Hayes's growling voice seemed to be speaking to me, asking "who's the sex machine to all the chicks..?" as though he were there, watching me, amused at my put-down.

'It's not me,' I thought, angrily. 'You fat shit-hole.'

I felt depressed. I missed Mary again and wondered if I should go up to her house and persuade her to come out. It was a bit late, though. I wasn't enjoying myself now and the music was beginning to get noisier. No matter how fine and handsome you may think you are as you pose in front of the mirror, as soon as a woman puts you down you feel the biggest prat on earth. That's why I went home.

Chapter 11

It is a summer evening. The sun is a huge disc of yellow in the clear blue sky. As I stand on the lawn and gaze across the misted, swooping hills, I can see the sea, like a distant green puddle, just two miles away to the south. The air is warm, and I can hear seagulls screeching and cackling above me as they pass over my head. I have just returned home from another hectic day working at the Café Majestic. How I hate that place. Mary's the only reason I stay there. I see her every day; I'm seeing her again tonight. That's why I'm feeling so happy.

I live with my parents in a sturdily built, white painted, ivy-covered cottage named, aptly, Sea View, in a green, quiet village called Chesterton, about five miles from the town. The place is a scattering of about thirty cottages, which include a Post Office and a public house (where I never go), just a mile off the busy main road. It's all very hopelessly peaceful; the kind of place to which bank managers retire.

I hear the 6.30 bus rattling and rumbling at the bus stop just down the road. I have to hurry now because I want to be out by seven. I walk around the garden to the back door and go inside. In the kitchen my parents are preparing the evening dinner. But it isn't initially for us; our cottage is small, but a popular guest house in the summer months and my mother has to cope with up to eight guests a week. They're pleased to see me, but busy. I say hello and go into my bedroom, next door. The room is really small, and dark. I have to turn on the light. It used to be my Dad's workshop, where he used to do odd jobs like mending the lawn mower and making home-made beer, until they realised the bedroom I was originally using was worth money if let to a guest, so after a swift re-decoration, I was moved into here. There's not much room to move about. Still, I've got it quite habitable with my posters of The Supremes and Stevie Wonder on the hastily-papered walls, and an old armchair in the corner.

I lie on the bed for just a moment. I feel tired. I've had a really exhausting day. I allow a drowsy sensation to seep over me just momentarily as I look up at my Stevie Wonder poster, feeling my eyelids grow heavy. Wonder holds his harmonica loosely in his long fingers and gazes upwards into blackness behind his dark glasses, his teeth smiling, his hair really short and crinkly. It's an early shot of him. He's about seventeen there, and already acclaimed by everybody, and making beautiful music. I'm a year older and all I do is wash-up dirty dishes. One day, though, I shall show the world what I can do. Just what that is, I don't know. One thing I realise; I can't do anything with my eyes closed...I jerk myself into motion and roll off the bed. I stand and stretch myself, then switch on my old battered Dansette record player beside the wall, put on a single, the Jackson Five's *I Want You Back* and leave the control arm up so it'll play over and over again, and turn the volume up as far as it will go so it will sound ridiculously loud and distorted.

The music blasts into the room. I pull off my jumper and tug off my shirt. With young Michael Jackson's piping urgent voice singing...*when I had you to myself*...I go out into the bathroom to wash. I wash my face, have a quick shave, and brush my teeth. I pass through the kitchen again. It's full of steam and smells and sounds of tinkling saucepans. Back in the bedroom I put on my Ben Sherman shirt, my nicely-faded Levi jeans, my dirty, soiled plimsolls, and I'm almost ready.

The record fades, finishes, rejects, then starts up again. The intro's so funky it makes me want to dance, but there's not enough room. Instead I bounce up and down like a pogo stick. It's really loud. At this moment my mother pokes her head around the door and tells me to turn down the 'noise' because she's trying to prepare dinner. She always seems to get into a flap. How can she work with all that 'noise' going on? I turn down the volume reluctantly. I guess I can be pretty inconsiderate sometimes. She says 'thank you' and tells me dinner will be ready soon. That's a good thing about living in a guest house: you get a good roast meal every day. It's roast lamb today and I eat it hastily.

I'm back in the bedroom again and my heart clangs when I think of the evening ahead. I'll be seeing Mary again and the prospect makes me feel both happy and nervous. Every time I see her, it's like a whole new experience. She knows I'm shy and feel uneasy sometimes, but she just doesn't care. I've been going out with her for a whole month now, so this must be it. We'll be together forever. She doesn't know, though, that she's the first girl I've ever been out with. Every time I see her I find myself smiling like an idiot. And at work, when I'm in the washroom, she creeps up on me and wraps her arms around me. On her days off, when I'm still working, she comes and sits in the cafeteria and just waits there, sometimes for hours, until I finish, the smiling one while all the jokers frown. Then she kisses me in front of everyone and they all look and nudge each other, smiling. But I just don't care. I feel so proud. Christ. I could go on forever...

The record, still playing, but a lot quieter now, fades, finishes, rejects, then starts again. The effect of that intro never seems to wane on me. It's all strings and bass and piano all playing together and sounding just great. Michael Jackson starts singing...*when I had you to myself*...once more, and I step over to the wardrobe, dancing at the same time, and grab my dirty parka hung over the wardrobe door. I pull it over my shoulders, push my arms into the thick, padded sleeves, wrap the entire bulk of it around my body, tug up the zipper, and here I am attired like some earth-bound spaceman. I take my long woollen scarf from one of the drawers and wrap it around my head several times and tie the loose ends into an enormous knot. I thrust my hands deep into my parka pockets and stand there. I look in the mirror. I stand and gaze at myself. I'm not at all good-looking. I wear horn rimmed glasses because I am myopic. My nose is big and there's a mole on my cheek and because I never wear a crash helmet, constant contact with the wind has made my short hair stick permanently upwards like the bristles of a scrubbing brush. I'll never know what Mary sees in me but then, isn't love blind?

I switch off the record player, open the door, pass through the steamy kitchen, shout goodbye to my parents, and now I am in the garden again. The sky is still a flawless blue, without a cloud in sight. The lawn is as green as a billiard table, and all the flowers in my mother's meticulous garden give the appearance of some summery paradise. A breeze is blowing, but only slightly. I reach the front of the cottage, where my scooter is parked. A car, almost a wreck, and covered in mud, rattles past. The sound of a labouring tractor in a distant field drifts on the warm summer air. I heave my scooter forward, so the two-legged stand springs back under the running-board with a clank. I lean it over slightly and prod the kick-start down once only. It starts. My face breaks into an idiot-smile. My scooter has started and the sun is shining, and down there in the town Mary is waiting. It seems everything is going my way....at least, that's how it feels.

Chapter 12

I arrived at Mary's bungalow, parked the scooter on the drive, as usual, and rang the front door bell. I heard the barking dogs, then the closing of doors within the place, then the slapping of slippered feet in the hall. The dogs barking sounded muted. They had been driven into the kitchen again, I thought, thankfully. They scared the wits out of me. I never trusted Alsatians. They had an unpredictable temperament, like panting one minute and growling the next. I could just imagine them tearing me apart, bone by bone and...Jennifer opened the door.

'Oh! Jack,' she said, looking neither pleased, nor displeased. She always seemed to maintain a bored, I-knew-it-would-be-you kind of look.

'Come on in.'

I followed her through to the sitting room and sat down in the armchair, my usual place. Already the room had become like a second home to me. I had grown accustomed to all its particular smells, moods and textures. For a month now I had been sitting in this very spot on curtain-drawn evenings after bringing Mary home after a walk to Cobham, or a drink in the pub, and sat talking to her mother, or watching television with a mug of tea poised on my knee.

'She'll be here in a minute.' Jennifer told me.

She sat down on the arm of the chair opposite and offered me a cigarette. 'You been working hard?' she asked.

'Yeah,' I said, taking a cigarette. 'Thanks.'

We lit up. She inhaled deeply.

'Don't your folks mind you smoking here?' I asked her.

She blew the smoke through her pursed lips slowly.

'No. why should they?'

I suppose it was a stupid question to ask as she wouldn't be smoking if they did. She was fifteen, after all, and it was illegal to smoke at that age. I was old enough, and smoked at home. My parents didn't say anything, though I knew they didn't really approve. We both sat in silence for a moment. Then I heard some muffled shouting from outside the room. Jennifer tutted loudly, her eyes looking up at the ceiling. 'She's having another row with mum,' she said.

I looked at her in surprise.

'What about?'

I heard thumping feet, rapidly approaching the door. Mary came into the room. She ignored me completely, and stood looking out of the window, sniffing loudly.

'You shouldn't keep swearing at mum,' said Jennifer, looking up to her.

'Piss,' she hissed between her teeth.

'You're gonna get it when dad gets home.'

'Piss off,' Mary retorted.

'It's your own fault,' said her sister, looking at her nails.

Mary crossed the room and sat sulkily in an armchair, sniffing. I remained quiet. I didn't know what was going on. I had seen her in moods like this before, and never knew quite what to do. She sat smouldering like some she-cat, her eyes burning through the window. Then she suddenly stood up, then left the room, slamming the door behind her. The front door slammed shut a second after. Jennifer stared at the door, then looked at me.

'You'd better go after her, Jack,' she said.

'What was it all about?' I asked.

Mrs Hawker came quickly into the room, looking angry.

'Where's the blessed girl gone?'

She saw me and smiled briefly.

'Hello Jack.'

'Hi,' I said, feeling confused.

'Oh, well,' she sighed, tiredly. 'Her father will know what to do when he gets home.'

She went out into the kitchen. The dogs started barking again. I looked at Jennifer.

'What's it all about?' I asked, standing up.

'She's a bitch,' she replied, with that bored expression on her face. 'Even though she's my sister, I have to say it.'

'What do you mean?'

'She's no good for you, Jack,' said Jennifer, looking suddenly concerned. 'I'd just forget about her.'

'But what's she done?' I asked, feeling confused, perplexed.

She paused.

'She was out all night with some bloke. She didn't get home 'til about two this morning. Dad was worried sick. She didn't phone or...'

'What do you mean...out with some bloke?' I butted in, feeling a strange pulling in my stomach. 'What bloke?'

Jennifer looked sorry for me.

'She goes with anyone,' she told me.

'She's going out with me,' I stated, realising I was sounding angry.

'Go after her,' Jennifer told me.

Standing on the doorsteps and looking down the lane I could see Mary walking purposefully, briskly, turning the corner at the bottom and disappearing behind the trees. I hurried to my scooter, started it and followed after her. I caught up with her and cruised along beside her on the wrong side of the road, slipping the clutch.

'Mary. Hang on a minute will you?' I pleaded. She wrinkled up her nose and looked away quickly as if I were an obnoxious smell.

'What have I done, for Christ's sake?' I bleated.

She had suddenly become untouchable and alien to me. I grappled in my mind for words to make her stop. If only I could talk to her. I suddenly became transparent, intangible, non-existent. A car's horn blared loudly as it passed me and I realised I must have been weaving all over the road while my head was full of sadness and bemusement over Mary. I crossed the road, stopped my scooter, pulled it up on its stand, then ran after her again. I grabbed her shoulder and she span around, glaring at me.

'Don't touch me,' she said.

'I've got to talk to you.' I almost whispered.

'Just leave me alone,' she retorted.

She continued walking and I followed after, like some homeless, helpless forlorn-looking, trotting-puppy-dog, its tail between its legs. I just couldn't bring myself to go. If only she would turn around and tell me everything was alright, like it was before. Was this the way all relationships ended; just hateful looks and non-communication? She had been the first girl I had felt anything for. I couldn't accept that she wasn't interested in me anymore. What was I to do? I was suddenly conscious of the fact that I was making a fool of myself in our town, on that pavement, another victim of the renowned Heart Breaker, another statistic in her little book of broken hearted victims. She turned her head and gave me a look that implied *What? Are you still here?* I wanted to stay with her forever, no matter what manner of hurt she piled on to me. She turned her head again and sniffed loudly, indignantly.

We reached the town. Not one word had been spoken, though my head was teeming with pleadings, spilling over with things to say to this girl I couldn't reach, no matter how fast I walked. I grabbed her arm in a sudden spurt of courage, attempting to spin her around to face me. She shook her hand free, not looking at me, instead walking ahead and treading on the heels of a couple of slow-walking laggards, apologising when they turned. Then she jumped upon a low wall in front of the church, balancing and teetering there, touching my head for support. She jumped down and came suddenly close, took my hand and rested her head upon my shoulder. A sensation of what must have been relief and joy rose within me momentarily. She pressed my fingers tightly together as I tried to act unperturbed, to look as though I knew she would come back all the time. My jubilation sank back to submerge level as soon as she spoke.

'It's all over between us,' she said matter-of-factly. 'It would never have worked anyway.'

'But Mary…' I said, pained, but she broke away and jumped awkwardly on to the church wall again, balancing there as though she were some absurd tight-rope walker, and the pavement, two feet below her, was some dark mysterious abyss.

'We could *make* it work,' I pleaded to her, 'couldn't we?'

She jerked her hips back and forwards as she tried to maintain her balance on the low wall, toppling, her arms making wild oscillations in the air, falling backwards with a gasp. She fell off on to a patch of daffodils, her long dark legs kicking, holding a hand over her mouth as she giggled helplessly. I stepped over

108

the wall and pulled her up, my mind reeling. This girl was crazy but Christ I couldn't help it, I loved her, craziness and all. I pulled her to her feet with a jolt, a forceful finality.

'You're not going to leave me,' I told her, feeling deep inside that everything I said was superfluous, that I was acting a part in some badly-written, melodramatic, Hollywood soap opera. She screwed up her face playfully.

'OK,' she said, but as soon as I relaxed my hold on her she darted away, over the wall, up the street and into a shop entrance, disappearing around a display window. I followed after her, through a short tunnel of plate glass and fashion clad mannequins. She darted again out into the street, colliding with a sports-jacketed youth, almost bouncing off his trunk-like body. He caught her shoulders and held her erect, recognising her. I stood still, hidden behind the glass wall of the shop's display. They stood there talking as I pretended to be looking at the shop display, looking, but not seeing the scantily-dressed mannequins in various designs of panty and bra. The youth still had his hands on her shoulders and I hated him for that. I knew they were talking about me. Mary looked over at me several times, smiling, expecting me to interject into their conversation and make a fool of myself, or get myself into a scrap with the youth, who was bigger than me. Something kept me from doing both of those things. I just stood there while the girl I loved tore me apart by just being so close and so far away at the same time. The predicament I was in must have been enacted a million times over by God-knows how many millions of people down through the ages, on every square-foot of land on the earth. We're all a population of mugs getting caught in that same old, old tired trap.

Mary grabbed the youth's arm, then steered him away up the street, pressing her body tightly against him. I ran out from the shop display and made to shout her name for the world to hear, to make her stop and walk right back, but the word just gagged in my throat, replaced by a painful pulling, like it used to do when I was about to cry as a kid. The very air about me seemed to press down upon me with a loud, humming heaviness, a droning that filled my ears. I was suddenly alone again, and it was a loneliness I just couldn't accept. A door had slammed shut against my back pushing me harshly into a bleak tundra of emptiness and heartache. I watched the youth and the girl I loved diminish in size as they made their way down the street. I just stood there hating myself for being so weak and spineless, for doing absolutely nothing. Why, that bastard had just walked off with my girl as easily as buying a cup of coffee in the Café Majestic. Now I had nothing, and a long way to walk back to my scooter...

I kept thinking of her that night. I tossed about in my bed, writhing this way and that way, unable to sleep. My tiny, dark bedroom compressed and pressed upon me with its narrow walls, its prison cell-like construction trapping me with a terrifying, mind-clotting claustrophobia. I felt I had to walk the streets or just hang about near her bungalow. Just to be near her... My tiny transistor radio perched on my pillow sent strains of tinkle-sound across the darkness, penetrating my ears and mind. Familiar songs and melodies tore me apart with a painful nostalgia. I banged my head upon the pillow, once, twice, three times, the music swirling and whirling inside my head. Could...could that record be the one? That very record, that very record was playing the night when...It faded away on a distorted, crackling interruption from a foreign channel, statically sizzling and spitting, phasing in and out, softly I cursed and moved the radio about. The music returned, hurting me once more. I groaned again and writhed this way and that. Rain suddenly splattered against the high window. I could hear the wind gusting ferociously against the thick walls of the house. Outside in the wild world it was cold and crazy, and there I was in my sweaty bed twisting and turning in the appalling darkness, the radio music filling my head with depression, though I didn't attempt to switch it off.

She was there, like a vision, she was there, looking down at me and smiling amidst the dwindling music, softly. Then she tossed her head and the shock of hair above her bare shoulders crackled like electricity. I opened my eyes and realised I must have fallen asleep very briefly, the radio hissing into my ear. A sudden remembrance shot through my body; of that afternoon, and my heart pained with a low, dull hurt. The voice of the untiring, garrulous DJ seemed suddenly more intimate and friendly. He was talking about Dateline, computer dating.

"There must be thousands like you" he told me, "all wanting companionship and love..."

Never. No-one on earth could have been as solitary and desolate as I was that night, I thought. The music continued to envelop me; street soul music of far-distant ghettos, gambolling and huffing, thumping drum and black harmonious heartbreak...*the love I lost was a sweet love.* All this seemed to belong to my own private universe of despair and isolation. I suddenly jerked bolt upright in the bed. The dark room compressed upon me so much that I tore the bedclothes away and stood frantically to grab my clothes, to dress, to go out and walk the streets or hang about near her home, to escape from that feeling of being squeezed and crushed in claustrophobic depression.

A sudden squall of rain against the window made the rashness of the moment unfulfilled. I stood there dark and shivering, the ghetto music still throbbing and needling, glissando-stringing and black-heart-aching around me. I climbed back into bed and hid beneath the sheets. I lay there, my eyes wide open, staring into the darkness, the music hidden behind my thinking. Her smiling face stared into my eyes, quietly. I could hear her voice. I remembered the way she held her cigarette in long and slender fingers. My eyelids grew heavy.

On the beach, laughing in the blustering devil-wind, running just ahead of the raging, crashing foaming waves that roared and splattered upon the pebbles, just ahead we ran. She screamed as the steaming mist showered and spat all around her; screamed and laughed shrilly, like a tiny child, stamping her foot. We skipped together ridiculous across the screaming rocks, our arms linked together, both clad in our heavy coats, her hair hanging sodden, like wet wire, down her neck and into her eyes. We walked for eternities along that deserted, growling beach until the stars speckled the universe, feeling both wet and warm. Her body was so fine and precious within my arms. I felt I might crush her, easily, without effort, crush her frail fragile body into dust with the coveted possession of her. I nuzzled my face into her hair as we stood against the moon. But she was suddenly as a mist...gone...gone.

I thumped the pillow in a strange, alien temper, screaming silently into the apocalyptic darkness, twisting and strangling the pillow in a fit of crazed anguish. The huge pulsating sun rose just beyond the hill. A vivid, Technicoloured Disney sky suddenly exploded with birds and singing. High on that hill we stood together. She walked away.

'You can't leave me,' I moaned pitifully.

She continued walking, her hands deep in her jeans pockets, not looking back. I ran after her. I grabbed her arm. She shrugged away, her eyes squinting with the sunlight rasping on to her face.

'I love you,' I told her.

She breathed a sigh of disbelief. 'Really?'

She sauntered away, stepping upon the endless universe. I ran after her again, confused and innocuous. She span around, her face lined with anger.

'Just piss off, will ya?'

'I don't understand you,' I told her.

She stood, the sun lighting up her hair like a million electric sparks, her body far out of reach again. I reached. She wrenched away.

'Don't you dare touch me.' She spat venomously.

'You're crazy.' I screamed.

She cried, sobbing, her hair trembling, her body quivering,

'I didn't mean it,' I choked.

I felt protective again. I wanted to hold and protect her. To see her crying pained me. All around us, far, far, far down below us the world and the cities grew and died. She sauntered away into the mists.

'Why..?' I cried to the radio, suspended somewhere between the hazy brilliant blue sky and the darkness of the sweltering bedroom.

Chapter 13

The Café Majestic was always our Sunday morning rendezvous for Alex and me. We thought that because we were up and doing something active, be it only sipping tea, we were showing others how full of life and energy we were. I couldn't sleep these nights anyway. It was a crisp and golden morning, a morning to make you walk tall on your toes and breathe the fresh intoxicating air deep into your lungs, to beat your chest with the joy of being alive. It was typically Sunday, the town being almost deserted. A seagull made its cackling, chuckling way through the air. A faded page of an abandoned newspaper scuttled and hovered on a cushion of air across the barren car park. Alex and I were sitting by the large panoramic window that scanned the car park, slurping tea and scratching our heads. There had been a party the night before and we were both feeling the aftermath. The café was empty and we both felt solitary and demented like two soldiers from the rigours of war, survivors, tattered with visions and ragged with headaches.

Alex sat in a huddled lump on the edge of his seat. He lifted his cup to take a further sip, considered for a second, his face devoid of all expression, then impulsively threw the steaming liquid on to the potted plants that decorated the low window ledge.

'Christ and shit,' he mumbled, his chin almost touching the table, replacing the cup clumsily onto the saucer with a clink. 'We actually pay them for this piss.'

He screwed his face up in disdain, glancing up at the large electric clock that never ticked.

'Christ. It's only nine o'clock.'

114

I felt slightly guilty for I had called him really early that morning and dragged him from his bed. I couldn't sleep again that night and was tired of pacing the bedroom carpet and circulating the town on my scooter as the sun rose from the other side of the world. His mother had told me to just go into his bedroom and get him up, and that's what I had done.

I shouldn't have shrieked, '*get up you 'orrible little man*' just like a sergeant major right into his ear, I suppose. I guess he was pretty sore with me. I offered him a cigarette and he took one and lit up, grimacing, rubbing his head.

'You should have seen the chick I was with,' he told me. 'Like a parrot.'

Good old Alex. I knew he wouldn't stay mad with me for long.

'God, I was *pissed*,' he exhaled, 'pissed as a *rat* but Christ, that woman had the biggest nose I've ever seen.'

'They call her "Rose the Nose" ', I explained to him. 'It's no wonder.'

'It was a pretty good party,' I said, even though I had gone home early, being unable to find a girl, or get into anything, being so preoccupied with thoughts of Mary, still.

Alex looked through the window, a look of deep concentration on his face. He took a long drag from his cigarette, almost smoking it down to the tip with that one drag. His parka was opened at the chest exposing his dirty, paint-covered tee shirt underneath.

'I can't even remember what I *did* last night,' he said, then his eyes opened wide, suddenly laughing. 'Yes I *do*. Yeah. That's right. I took her into this room, the chick with the nose, y'know? She was breathing all heavy and whispering these crazy things into my ear. I was getting near it, had her on the carpet with her tights

115

and knickers around her ankles, then I blew it all by saying to her "what are you breathing heavy for? You got asthma or something?"'

'What happened then?' I asked. I wanted to see the whole movie.

'She just stiffened like a corpse,' Alex explained, incredulous, as though he couldn't believe, himself, what he had done the night before. 'Everything just went...phuuuuut,' he said, rasping through his lips, making a farting sound and gesticulating with his fingers a balloon suddenly deflating and shrivelling into nothing. Only Alex would have dared do such a thing. Only he.

The simple fact that Alex was our unofficial and uncelebrated leader, had gone unrecognised for so long, the matter had become obsolete and unimportant anyway. I, for one, would nominate him, without any regret whatsoever, for such a coveted position. I guess we all wanted the prestige of being the 'leader'. We would stand around the darkened windows of the fish and chip shop arguing who could do the craziest things to prove our sovereignty, while Alex would just stand in the shadows eating his chips hungrily, or recline, long and languid, across his scooter, his hands behind his head, his plimsolls resting on the headlight. We boasted that we could do 'wheelies', ride around the car park standing on the saddle, ride through the town in the midst of a freezing winter without a shirt, emerge from fights unscathed, while Alex remained quiet of the fact that he during the time he had lived in digs while he went to art college, in some back-street, damp-walled bed-sit, had spent all his money at the weekend buying us drinks and then had to go without food for days on end. That in itself was something to respect; most of us lived cheaply and pampered at home, and hadn't even been further than Baybridge. Alex was, in those days, our epitome, a mould in which we, like molten plastic, poured ourselves in, shaping our own futile lives, to be just like him, coming out with mannerisms like mass-produced clichés. It was like that for me, anyway. He was the direction to wild intoxications, of stormy night parties with the constant reminder that 'life was for living', for getting crazed, pissed, lost, found again...

As our shortening days tumbled upon us, our careers and ambitions still hidden obscure behind our fun and games, Alex remained unchanged, still sucking cigarettes and wondering what all the fuss was about. The pantomime-realisation of our reckless libertine ways came to us individually, like Russian Roulette, until the lucid fact that youth and moments of time and all that went with it, was slowly draining from us, leaving us with nothing but a puzzled concept of life and a mock interpretation of what we were going to do next. No. Alex never changed. So engrossed in my thinking, I was, I didn't notice Jason Jones walk into the cafeteria, buy a cup of tea and pad silently in his Doctor Martin boots between the aisles of chairs and tables towards us.

'Hello Alex, hello Jack,' he said.

I looked up, and Alex and I nodded at him respectfully. He sat down beside me.

'Couldn't you sleep either?' Alex asked him'

Jason was the hardened leader of the town's skinheads, the alternative faction of the town. He was a good-looking youth who had a regular shave on his head, giving him the appearance of an emancipated coconut. He had shaky hands, especially when he held something small like a guitar plectrum or a box of matches, he spoke peacefully and always seemed to be covered by a thin layer of brick-dust because he was a brick layer, and was an enforced friend of the populace. He was older than us, was a lot stronger, went to church, sang in the choir, helped run a local village youth club, was the most versatile jazz guitarist I had ever heard. But he also kicked dust-bins over, hurled people he didn't like through shop windows which shivered into confetti upon impact, bought expensive rounds of drinks for entire-pub-loads of people, and called everyone 'shit houses'....a bit of an ecclesiastical thug, if there was such a thing.

'And how are you, Alex?' he asked.

'Fine, thank you, Jason,' said Alex, almost with reverence.

'And you, Jack?'

'Fine, thank you, Jason,' I replied, likewise.

He regarded us for an instant, then began to sip his tea. His head was fair and freshly shaven, shiny and fleshy white, like the downy body of a bee. His Ben Sherman shirt was black and white chequered, freshly washed and ironed, as were his slightly faded Levi jeans. Altogether, along with his braces, he was a quite respectable skinhead.

He was also a good friend, though we feared him. He had this strange, unexpected tendency to suddenly turn against us, to kick us around with those Doctor Martin boots, but then, on other occasions, he would buy us drinks, solve our problems and lend us money. I liked Jason. He understood things.

'You really ought to get yourselves organised,' said Jason, suddenly. 'have you got a job yet, Alex?'

Alex shrugged his shoulders.

'Well. Get one.'

'Yes, Jason,' said Alex.

We remained silent for what seemed an eternity. Jason produced a packet of Senior Service and we all lit up.

'I like your parka, Alex,' said Jason finally, 'I want it. How much do you want for it?'

Alex looked surprised. He had had the coat for years, had it washed a hundred times, cleaned his sparking plugs on it, blown his nose in the sleeves, torn one of the pockets off. To see Alex without that ragged, billowing shapeless garment would have been unthinkable. Still, his constant state of poverty made him do some pretty surprising things sometimes.

'Three quid?' he asked expectantly.

Jason leaned over, pulled some crumpled pound notes from his back jeans pocket and tossed them on the table. Alex quickly unzipped, shucked and pulled off his coat, emptying the pockets of an oily rag, a spark plug, a few pennies and a letter to Vanessa he'd forgotten to post, and bundled it quickly into Jason's arms, as if he might suddenly change his mind, or regret the transaction. It amazed me the things he did when he was fed up with being broke. Jason rolled the parka into a ball and placed it on the floor, by his chair. Alex sat shivering there in just his dirty, paint-splattered tee-shirt, looking quite white and unhealthily thin.

A lone Sunday morning driver sped around the car park, his tyres burning the tarmac. We all turned our heads to watch the car going fruitlessly round and round, wondering if we knew the driver.

'Let's see this trick of yours then, Alex,' said Jason.

'Huh?' said Alex.

'The trick with the matchstick.'

'Oh! That trick.'

The trick was performed with long, clever fingers, a trick that had been rehearsed and rehearsed again. He

119

did it in moments of sudden inspiration, or just when he felt like it. It was done with closed eyes and a rocking head, a trick that was claimed as miraculous. It had won him acclaim from all four corners of the earth, to distant islands and forgotten archipelagos, a trick that was admired by millions. The trick was the extinguishing of a burning match stick in the cavity of his closed mouth, not quite as stupendous as I tended to make out. (I do go over the top sometimes), but it was a good trick all the same. I would watch him perform this minor feat with eyes wide and mouth open. I had tried to do it and had burnt my teeth. Alex took a box of Swan Vestas from the table and selected a match. The intense quiet of the morning seemed to grow even quieter. The empty café seemed to become a vast wasteland of sheer expectancy. We waited with bated breath. A bead of sweat glistened on Alex's brow. We waited.

'It's not much of a trick really,' he stated.

Jason just looked at him silently. Then his left eyelid twitched just a little bit, always a bad sign. Alex struck the match with a rasping sound and held up the flame for us to see. He opened his mouth wide, inserted the flaming match, closed his mouth, opened it again, and bought out the match, extinguished, and smoking a bit.

'Very good,' said Jason, obviously impressed, then very cool.

'Now do it with what's left in the match box.'

'I hardly think so. I'd blow my head off.'

Jason leaned sideways and pulled another crumpled note from his Levis pocket. That was another good thing about him; he had no hassles about throwing his money around.

'There you are, Alex,' he said, laying the tempting note out on the table, ironing it out with his hand. 'The pound's yours if you can do it.'

Alex looked at the money, then at Jason, took a long drag from his cigarette and crushed it out in the cheap plastic ashtray.

'Make it two,' he said.

Another note was pulled from Jason's pocket, laid flat, ironed out on that blue Formica table top; two grass-green slips of paper, enough to buy pints of Bitter and southern Comfort, or cigarettes, or even some food. To Alex, together with the three pounds for the parka, it was a fortune. He looked at the money with those tired eyes, and the sight of those two notes seemed to register in his pupils with a strange reflected twinkle. To Alex, the money had become translucent, transparent, and through those frosty windows he saw a copious world of riches; a fresh packet of cigarettes tightly packed in cellophane, a slightly spilling glass of Bitter, freshly poured, slid towards him on that shiny bar-top down the Nine Stars, a meal of fish and chips, steaming and piping hot, full of nourishment and wrapped in newspaper. He gave the money yet another covetous look, and sure enough, he was cajoled, and cozened. He shot Jason a look that told he had made up his mind, lit another cigarette with a shaking hand then threw the matchstick into the ashtray.

'Alright,' he said. 'I'll do it.'

He rested his cigarette in the ashtray, then picked up and rattled the matchbox to hear the contents. There were at least thirty matches in that box. He swallowed hard and picked up his cigarette and pulled another inhalation. Again he put it back in the ashtray. Then he slid the tray from the matchbox and tipped the matches into the palm of his hand, blowing thick smoke from his lips as he did so. He grabbed and bunched the matches together and held them tightly, their red heads upwards, his hands shaking alarmingly. He took a loose match and struck it, then held it for us to see. The flame danced and bulged and he considered it for a second. Then he touched it against the bunch of matches in his other fist, and it rasped stutteringly, flaring into a little ball of fire. With a grumbling sound, Alex pushed the lot into his mouth. His teeth lit up a dull orange incandescence, like a smiling Halloween pumpkin, his eyes wide with animal fear, smoke seeping in little whorls from his nostrils. It was over in a second. Alex withdrew the fused-together, clinker-like-headed bunch of dead matches from his mouth and tossed it into the ashtray. He rubbed his nose, his face breaking into a smile, grabbed the money from the table and stuffed it triumphantly into his pocket.

It was in a more confidential, problem-solving limelight I saw Alex. He would always listen when I needed someone to talk to, to pour out my troubles. He seemed to be the only one who cared, who took any interest. May be it was because we were both in the same predicament; both hurt and disillusioned by love, that he seemed to know the right answers and solutions when I needed them. And as he was my best mate, he was always the one I called on when he couldn't afford petrol to run his scooter, the one I lent money to that wouldn't be reimbursed. When the trees were being torn and whipped into distortion by chilling winds, or when the red sun hung large and shimmering in the silver sky, I would have these problems, and up to Alex's house I would go. Alone, up the billiard green hill I'd ride, into the peaceful, sprawling suburbia where his parents lived, park my scooter on the gravel, and walk up his path. Then I would knock on the door.

Alex would answer my rasping and stand tall and scruffy in the doorway. He would have been just sleeping, and would stand there rubbing his eyes, or he would be covered in paint, dressed in his ragged jeans and knotted jumper. Sometimes his mother would answer the door and she would ask me in, and Alex would be stretched out on the front room floor, his head propped against the leg of the armchair, a cigarette poised between his lips, watching *Tomorrow's World*, or he would be drying his hair with a hair dryer. I would sit in his front room and his mother would bring me a piece of incredible cake and a large mug of rich, streaming cocoa. Then Alex would scramble up and say, 'Let's go, then,' and he would drag himself in an old, disgustingly-scruffy parka, wrap a long scarf around his neck as though lagging a pipe, and we would go out and ride to the Youth Club in the blinding winds. When his parents were both away, the throbbing, shrieking sounds of his old record player would fill the empty road of his suburbia. Of course, it was mostly Motown records he played. His collection was rather sparse, however, only having a scratched, coverless Jimmy Ruffin album, and a few celebrated singles, from an ancient Four Tops to an early Mary Wells. Alex would stand in the doorway, amidst that maelstrom of loud sound, and ask me into the deafening bedroom. I would sit there and Alex would point with moist eyes, and lean and nod to some enigmatic verse or a familiar, predictable Motown riff... *I'll be there...the empty side-walks on my own are not the same...don't walk away...take your love away, I'll turn to stone...* To Alex the songs were his own private pictures, a crude language of nostalgic depression. The music could elucidate his innermost feelings and make them almost unbearable. In every one of those records, it was Alex, and I, who were being hurt, who were walking sad and alone on a Detroit side-walk, who were cold and empty, like statues in a park… and our sadness for the loves of our life, by just listening to that music, in that room, would be exaggerated to bombastic proportions.

It was Vanessa, acting her part in Alex's mind when those records were being played. And, finally when the record player was switched off, he'd light up another cigarette and tell me all about her, and I'd tell him my problems concerning Mary. No matter how intense I felt about it, he always brought some sanity to my rather dewy-eyed infatuation with heartache...

'I saw her again today, Alex. I was riding through town and she looked at me...d'you think it means anything?'

'What d'you mean, d'you think it means anything?' Course it doesn't mean anything.'

'But she looked at me.'

'She was probably thinking what an asshole you are.'

'D'you think so?'

And so on...

Chapter 14

Our scooters made their rattling way down the steep, rutted dusty track that led to the secluded beach and the sea at Devil's Dive, a privately-owned cove set back from the natural course of the coastline, appearing as though it had been shaped by a giant mouth taking a ravenous bite from the land and devouring it. We hadn't been there before because the owners normally chained and padlocked all the entrances securely, though many people still got there by walking along the beach from Cobham, five miles away. They were mostly holiday-makers and ramblers with nothing better to do. It was just another beach, after all, being less accessible and thus more secluded than the rest. We were only heading there because we had heard a party was going on. We hadn't been invited. Alex was riding on the back of me, his long woollen scarf wrapped round his neck and a large bottle of wine under each arm. He leaned forward, his short sun-bleached hair swept back by the wind, his mouth close to my ear.

'Hey. Just look at Owen,' he yelped. 'He knocked back a full bottle of wine half an hour ago, now look at him.'

Owen's scooter was bobbing and swerving.

I accelerated and rode up level with him, steering and weaving around the deeper ruts. I shouted across, keeping my eyes on the rough surface of the track.

'Hey. You'll ruin your suspension riding like that, man. You OK?'

He smiled across like a sodden Cheshire cat, taking his glazed eyes from the track just a little too long, then jolting stiffly as he bumped over a large stone. He raised an arm like a cowboy breaking-in a wild horse at a rodeo.

'You bet I'm OK,' he laughed.

The track levelled off as we reached the beach. Owen suddenly careered into a high mound of shingle, blowing and cursing and rolling over. He lay motionless for an instant, but recovered quickly. He sprang to his feet, tottered slightly, heaved his capsized, still-spluttering scooter from the ground, remounted and continued as before, waving his arm to show he was unharmed.

The sea was near-motionless, and green, like a vast undulating sheet of dark, deep cellophane. Tiny fishing boats could be seen on the thin line of the horizon, far away. The sun was a large red semi-circular disc suspended in its process of setting, half above the glittering water and half on its way to the other side of the world. We parked beside some dusty cars by a fence, apart from Owen who was now attempting to ascend another extensive mound of shingle, his engine revving loudly, his legs kicking out to keep balance as his wheels sank deeper, almost immovably, spitting sprays of grit from his spinning back wheel. Matthew went to help him out. Raymond put his hands deep into his parka pockets.

'So where's this party?' he asked no-one in particular, looking along the beach.

'Give us a chance,' Gary retorted, scratching his nose. He had been the one who had told us about the party. He felt responsible, somehow, for the success or failure of that evening. 'We haven't even looked yet.'

The beach seemed barren and desolate. The wind was beginning to blow and the sun finally slipped behind the horizon. The sound of Owens's labouring engine slowly died away, like a switched-off electric saw, as he and Matthew were now attempting to pull his scooter out of its lodged position in the dunes.

'Sssshhhh,' Alex rasped suddenly, his fingers pressed to his pursed lips, staring intently ahead of him, his two wine bottles clinking together under his arm. Approximately fifty yards further along the beach was a high ridge. Beyond this, straining our ears over the incessant sound of the waves breaking on the shore, we could faintly hear a girl's shrill laughter, and the sound of thin, tinny music wafting on the wind.

'It's over there,' he stated, pointing towards the ridge.

We started walking laboriously across the beach, our plimsolls sinking in and crunching into the shingle. Raymond turned and shouted to Matthew and Owen, cupping his hands over his mouth, still stepping backwards.

'Come on, hurry up. We think we've found it.'

They had only just pulled the scooter from the dune and Gary was now attempting to restart it for Owen so he could ride over to the fence to park it. Matthew stood with his hands on his hips, shouting: 'Can't you lot bloody wait for us, or something?'

'Well come on then, hurry up,' Alex shouted back. 'Bloody pissing about.'

As we drew still nearer to the ridge, a head appeared just above it. A curly-haired youth was walking towards us and as he came nearer his body seemed to grow down from his neck. He ascended the shingle, then fully exposed, plodded towards us, looking down at his treading feet. He looked surprised when Alex spoke to him.

'Hey, mate. Are we right in assuming there's a party over there?'

The youth seemed to be quite nervous. No doubt he thought we were going to suddenly kick him to the ground or something.

'Yes. You're right,' he told us, his eyes darting back along the beach to the ridge. 'But you haven't been invited, have you?'

'I have,' said Gary, picking his nose, pushing a finger so far up his nostril it almost disappeared.

'So have I,' I said, 'been invited,' my teeth chattering in the wind.

'What's all this, 'you haven't been invited shit?' said Alex, dryly, grabbing the youth's thick-wool jumper, pulling him to him, making him suddenly shudder, then tense up. 'A party is a party, after all, and everyone is "invited".'

'If you say so,' the youth giggled nervously.

'I'll let you come to *my* party,' said Alex releasing his hold, 'if I ever have one.'

'Yes. That's very kind,' murmured the youth, pressing his jumper down, then pointing. 'The party's just over there.'

We reached the ridge and looked down. There was a large fire, crackling and hissing, the high flames leaning on the breeze. We could feel the heat warm against our faces.

There were about thirty people there, all about our age, sitting around the fire, some hunkered down, hands cupped over the flames to keep warm. Empty beer bottles and Coke cans were strewn around them. The Beach Boys' 'I Get Around' was playing thinly from a cheap-looking cassette player. A large plastic bag lay by the fire, was full of bread rolls, and packets of hamburger meat, which was a good thing because I was feeling hungry. We slid down the bank of the ridge and sat there feeling the warmth of the fire and the eyes of

128

the crowd upon us. Looking around me I recognised the faces instantly. I used to be one of them. They were all from Comprehensive School; all very brainy and all very boring. I used to go around with them when I was there. That was until I attained only three GCE O Levels in the exams, and was advised by a bored careers officer to leave. I got the job at the Café Majestic, bought a scooter, met Alex, and ended up like this; gate-crashing their parties.

It was incredible to think that these old friends were still there, still at the old school, now in the upper-sixth form, probably collecting their A Level certificates by now, like philatelists collect stamps. I seemed to have gone a long way, but nowhere, since the days I used to enjoy these mild affairs, discussing exams, algebraic formulae and the Theories of Newton. All those sleepless nights with my head propped over opened text books, burning the midnight oil, came back to me for just an instant. Was it really a year ago? If I remembered correctly, we never liked intruders at our 'parties', they were nearly always very private, exclusive affairs for the chosen elite. I felt very out of place, and very unwelcome. Those staring, wide eyes proved my suspicions right. Worse still, some one had turned the music off, so we were all sitting in a strange fire-crackling silence. Finally Alex waved his wine bottles in the air.

'Anyone got a corkscrew?'

A tall, shivering youth flared up from behind the fire, flushed with anger and pointing a jabbing finger at us. It was Peter Moss-Andrews, now the school's head boy, and a real pain in the ass, if I remember rightly.

'You bloody lot can clear off for a start. No-one invited you. You're not going to mess up this party like you did the last one.'

'You call this a "party"?' Alex retaliated, staring at him coldly.

'This is my parent's private land, and you had better get off it fast.'

'Piss off,' Gary replied, to our amazement, not normally being the one for such conclusive statements.

'How dare you?' breathed Moss-Andrews, looking like a devil, long nosed and reddened amidst the flames of the fire. He seemed to dance and spin there, stamping his foot and spitting with anger, forever the spoilt brat.

I couldn't, for the life of me, see what all the fuss was about. We were doing no harm whatsoever. It was only when I remembered the other party of theirs we gate-crashed that I understood their reason for not wanting us there. It was at Moss-Andrews's rambling country house about a month before and we had all been pretty drunk. Gary had vomited over their carpet and I had broken an antique vase, somehow, dancing like an idiot all over the place. It was worth a few hundred quid apparently. They had put it in a spare room for safety, but I had gone in there thinking it was the loo. Anyway, they couldn't prove it was me who broke it, which was the main thing. Alex shouldn't have urinated in the punch when no-one was looking, then sat and watched them drink it, I suppose. I guess we had been pretty disgusting. No wonder they didn't want us there.

Just then Matthew and Owen appeared at the crest of the ridge, supporting the youth we had seen earlier between them. He seemed to be in great pain, his head lolling loosely, a trickle of blood visible from his nose, down his chin.

'Good God,' said Moss-Andrews, aghast. 'You've not been fighting?'

We all looked up at the trio in a shocked silence.

'It's alright, really,' said the youth, weakly. 'It was completely my fault.'

'What have you been up to for Christsakes?' Alex asked, in a serious tone.

My two friends helped the youth down the bank and laid him down carefully. Owen fell down on his backside. He was pretty drunk.

'Owen rode over him on his scooter,' Matthew explained. 'We were just doing a bit of dirt-tracking across the beach when this guy suddenly loomed up and we, well, we ploughed right over him.'

'Christ,' said Alex, 'is he alright?'

'Of course he's not alright,' spat Moss-Andrews, crunching over to us. He was pretty angry. 'After I've taken him to hospital I'm going to fetch the police.'

'No. I'm alright, Peter,' said the battered youth, 'there's no need for the hospital.'

'Christ, Owen,' said Gary. 'You had the entire beach to yourself. How'd you manage to knock down one bloody guy with all that space around you?'

'Shit,' he retorted, trying to focus his eyes on him. 'He got in the bloody way.'

'Wherever you bastards go, there's trouble,' Moss-Andrews groaned, attempting to lift his friend up. 'Come on, let's get you to the hospital.'

'No, Peter,' said the youth. 'It's alright, really. I'm alright.'

All the others had now gathered around us, some kneeling around their friend, eyeing us spitefully. One twee, thin girl, who apparently remembered me from school days came up and pleaded with me to go away.

'Ooooohhh, Jack,' cried Owen, mimicking her voice. 'Who's your friend?'

'Shaddup,' I told him. 'You've caused enough trouble already.'

131

Moss-Andrews sighed heavily, resting his hands on his hips. 'Are you bastards going to go now?'

Matthew grabbed his jacket lapel harshly, making him jolt stiffly.

'Look. Don't call me a bastard, you big *shit*.'

Moss-Andrews stared into his face, his eyes dilating. Then he tore his lapel away from Matthew's grip, and brushed past him up the bank.

'There he goes,' said Alex, cutting into the wine bottle cork with a penknife. 'Off to the piggies like a little diddums.'

All the others were just standing around us, staring at us glumly. It was quite disconcerting. Gary started cooking a hamburger on a piece of stick against the fire. Owen fell asleep, snoring softly. Then we heard Moss-Andrews' Triumph Spitfire roar distantly up the hill. We watched until he reached the main road, saw his indicator flash on, off, on, off, on, off, then nose into a slight crevice, turn sharply at the junction and burble down the main road towards the town. He was going to fetch the police. I suppose it was pride that made us stay there. Anyway, it was interesting to see what the outcome would be. I doubted if the police would come anyway. They had enough to do without having to deal with party gatecrashers.

By now the party had split into two factions; the original people, and us. We were doing better though; we had the bag of rolls and hamburgers, and were making a good job of devouring them. The party crowd from school were now completely ignoring us, sitting at the opposite side of the fire. But the music resumed and we were drinking our way through Alex's second bottle of wine. It was beginning to seem like a party after all. Just then Owen sat bolt upright from his drunken slumber.

'Hey,' he piped. 'I can't have the piggies coming down here. My bike's not taxed. They're bound to look over our bikes if they come down here.'

Anyway being confronted by the police had become not altogether a very comforting proposition. We decided to leave. Halfway up the hill we met the patrol car on its way down. The police officer, a broad shouldered, thick-jowled gum-chewer leaned out of his window, his sorrel eyes cold and exact, looking at us unblinkingly, his cap tilted over his forehead.

'Where's the trouble, then,' he drawled.

We remained motionless on our shuddering scooters, expecting the tirade of abuse and handcuffs any second.

'They're down there,' said Alex, suddenly, leaning over me uncertainly and pointing towards the beach. 'You'd better get down there quick officer, sir, they're all drugged up to the eyeballs, and fighting, and doing all kinds of terrible things. We've never seen anything like it.'

The police officer's hard eyes opened wider in their sockets.

'Really? Good lord, I'd better get down there.'

We watched the patrol car slither and float down the darkening track like an exhausted rocket returning to earth, saw the policeman, very small and uniformed, leap out onto the beach, then make his wary way across the beach towards the slowly-dying fire.

Chapter 15

Alex was pretty unlucky when it came to scooters. They seemed to fall apart on him. It was due, mainly, to a lack of maintenance; a complete disinterest in the mechanics of the things. As long as they got him about, got him to where he wanted to go, that's all he cared about. In a moment of inspiration, while at Art College one day, he decided to have his trusty scooter serviced. He took it to local garage. All that week we looked forward to its return, when it would be competently overhauled, by professional, spanner-wielding fingers, fully tuned and sweetly running. To Alex's horror, when he returned to the garage to collect it, after much bus-waiting, pavement-treading and ride-hustling, he found both the scooter and the mechanic gone, never to be seen again. After much letter writing and heated argument, the insurance company finally paid up, and with some extra money lent to him by his parents, Alex got what he always wanted: a brand new scooter.

It was a winter night, with the heaviest fall of snow we had experienced in years. Matthew and I were in the Youth Club, hovering over the old rattling convector heater as though our very lives depended on it. It was that cold. The juke box was flickering with a loose bulb somewhere deep within its womb, playing *My Cherie Amour*, my favourite record at the time. The place was crowded. Matthew and I were waiting for Alex. For weeks now he had been telling us how wonderful his new scooter would be, how fast, how sleek, how superior it would be to anything we had ever seen before. How enthusiastic and excited he had been about it. We could hardly wait to see it. And, here he came, making his way on foot through the storm across the car park. He saw us looking through the window, and waved at us, almost blotted away by the tumbling dollops of snow, attired in an oversized, frost-rimed, brown great-coat that skirted the ground. We ran out to meet him, to behold the new machine.

'Where is it?' we chorused.

'I thought you were going to bring it over tonight,' I told him.

'I did,' he replied, 'it's over there.'

He pointed a long, cold finger to the place by the wall where we always parked our scooters. And there it was, parked next to mine, immaculate new, and apart from the snow, spotlessly clean, twinkling with little sparks of newness, like in a picture in a glossy magazine. The new scooter.

'But it's beautiful,' I exhaled.

His face broke into a broad smile.

'It sure is,' said Matthew, though we could both sense that he was feeling slightly jealous. 'You'll have the only Vespa SS180 in town.'

He nodded his head in agreement.

'Yup.'

'Christ, but what a bike,' I enthused, 'I can't get over it.'

There it was, being gradually covered in snow, smelling of new leather and clean-as-a-whistle engine, its exhaust pipe going *ping* as it gradually cooled. Full of power, it must have been, beneath those bulging metallic-blue, thickly polished, scratch-free panels.

'C'mon then Jack,' said Alex, turning up his coat collar against the snow. 'Let's take it for a spin.'

'But it's got to be run-in,' I told him. 'Hasn't it?'

'Doesn't matter'

'Does.'

'Oh come *on*, you old woman.'

Matthew stood waving at us like a forgotten soldier in the tumbling air as we meandered through the dunes. I could feel the vibrancy there between my legs as I sat on the virginal pillion seat behind Alex, the tight power-packed engine going *ting-ting-ting-ting* through its still-clean exhaust pipes. We splashed on deep-treaded tyres across the slush-covered car park to the street. Then Alex wrenched back the throttle and we shot forward, back wheel spinning at breath-taking speed halfway to the traffic lights before I had time to think.

'And that's only third gear,' my friend cried. We rode past Vanessa's house three times, just in case she came out and saw us, then sped around the town, proud and untouchable, skating over the ice, skidding sideways, spitting blue puffs of exhaust smoke, whizzing up the open road and cruising effortlessly back again. A motorcyclist rumbled past us, dark and embittered, so we chased him, through the sleeping streets, under bridges, through tunnels, through creepy, haunted woods, across the blinding, snow-speckled countryside, and back to the Youth Club.

Needless to say, after a few short months in Alex's haphazard care, the scooter was a mess. He covered it in stickers, had a furry back-rest screwed cock-eyed on the back, seized the engine up for a pastime, and repainted it regularly. We used to close our eyes and take bets, before he arrived, on what colour it had become since we last saw it. Alex was an expert with the paint brush; it was just that he couldn't afford a whole pot of paint and used any spare pigment he found lying around in the garage. On many of our mass-excursions, or on a quick trip to Cobham, there'd be a loud clatter, then a splintering of metal, then a screeching of tyres. We'd all stop and look behind us, and there'd be Alex, kneeling in the gutter, obscured by dust, picking up one of his side-panels, or his exhaust pipe. Pieces flew off it like it had been especially constructed for a circus clown routine. But that same unpredictable Vespa always remained fast. It would whisper past us along misty-mountain motorways, scream past us down midnight-sleeping streets to leave us jerking and throbbing in its undertow, choking and sneezing in its dust. He was notorious, infamous, even unpopular for his inability to ride his scooter safely, in a way that would not attract the gimlet eye of the safety-conscious constabulary. He would speed, weave, lean against the air, maintain constant speeds manoeuvring hairpin bends, crash into walls, fall off, fall into ditches, and ride home at night feeling stupidly drunk and sleepy. Then one day, to my sheer horror and discomfort, I learned that that same clattering, maniac-jinxed machine also boasted a total lack of brakes, and I almost paid the price with my life for that snippet of education.

Chapter 16

It happened one hot summer day. I had finally terminated my employment at the Café Majestic and was, therefore, out of work, hanging loose, not in a particular hurry to find a job, and enjoying myself, just like Alex. I had called for him quite early and dragged him from his sheets. Then we had gone into the Café Majestic for a cup of tea, yawning and staring blindly through the window. Then we rode down to Cobham on Alex's scooter and sat on the harbour wall watching the holidaymakers jostle past us in their mild confusion, studying their clothes and mode of ambulation. There was an acute shortage of eligible girls at that time of the morning, we both agreed. We slowly got bored. Then we remembered that Jonathon Cruft was also out of work and would probably be at home. We rode once again along the seafront then made for the town.

Jonathon was as tall as Alex, strong, very good-looking in a tanned, Maltese kind of way, had black hair and rather big hands. He always seemed rather aloof from the rest of us in that he stayed in more than usual, had a sarcastic sense of humour, slightly taciturn and had his own directions to aim for anyway. He would often gaze at us with a vacant expression, say, 'what a drag'. He would get drunk just like the rest of us, but would then go home and wouldn't be seen again for weeks on end. He would offer his cigarettes around freely, make fun of us, overtake us on the motorway, call us names when we couldn't afford to buy him drinks, then take his ageing dog for long slow walks across the playing fields. Jonathon was a good friend. We were always pleased to see him. So that sunny-yellow, easy morning we stood in front of his council flat door, banging loudly on the frosty-glass portion, waiting for his arrival, or awakening. His bedroom curtains had been drawn, so we expected him to still be in bed. He was. We waited and looked at the door. We heard a shuffling and a low moaning. And then the door opened slowly. Jonathon stood there in his red underpants.

'Oh!' he uttered hoarsely, scratching his head. 'What's the time then?'

'Ten o'clock, or thereabouts,' Alex told him, leaning against the door frame.

'Oh!' he repeated with a bored expression.

'Can we come in?' asked Alex.

'Sure,' said Jonathon, rubbing an eye. 'I'll just get dressed. You can put a record on if you want.' He went back into his bedroom.

Jonathon only had three LPs: Stevie Wonder's *Greatest Hits, With the Beatles,* and *Tommy.* We didn't bother putting them on. We found his cigarette packet and pinched two of his cigarettes instead. We looked through the window at some children on the grass playing football, puffing on those first cigarettes of the morning, (we couldn't afford to buy any) and planned what we were going to do next. Jonathon came back into the room dressed in a pair of heavily-patched Wranglers, worn-out plimsolls and old tee shirt.

'Bloody Krauts,' he said, 'pinching my fags.'

Yes, Jonathon was completely dissatisfied with the way his life was passing him by, was disgruntled with the fact that there were no opportunities for good, career-boosting jobs in the town apart from a small factory and a brewery. He was adamant he would leave the area one day and start off again somewhere completely different, miles away. He was bored with routine and wearing parkas, and, much more serious, he was plagued with misfortune and bad luck, though I always felt he was destined for success, somehow. His first scooter had literally fallen to pieces. He had bought a new one but smashed it up regularly. The side-panels always seemed to fall off, the paint-work almost obliterated by scratches and rust. All this had nothing to do with lack of maintenance or bad driving; it was all down to, 'bad luck and fate'. That was his theory, anyway.

'My scooter's going really well,' said Jonathon, then pausing to light a cigarette. 'In fact, it's going so well I think I'll sell it...'

After a cup of coffee, and a few more of his cigarettes, we ventured out into the backyard. Jonathon went into the garage to fetch his scooter, and then out he rattled, juddering and belching dense black smoke. All GTs rattled, but not like his; it sounded like broken crockery being rotated in a cement mixer.

'Where are you going, then?' he asked, revving his throttle harshly to prevent the engine dying on him.

'Back down to Cobham?' said Alex, an expectant look on his face.

Jonathon just shrugged his shoulders.

'Yeah. Sure,' he said.

One trip on the back of Alex had been enough for me, for one day. I didn't like to tease death that often. I hated riding pillion, with anyone. I would bite my lip, look up to the sky and cry to the gods, or God, or whatever, and seethe and swoon with clenched teeth...shit...this guys crazy...we're never gonna come out of this corner...we're not gonna...uh, and so on. It was all due to bad nerves, of course, and mental pictures of me broken and bleeding against the kerb stone. Anyway, Jonathon wasn't erratically crazy like Alex, so on the back of him I felt relatively 'safe'.

The sun was warming the sky, a globular blaze of fire suspended in magenta space. Traffic was congested, jam-packed-motionless, all the way to Cobham, bonnet nudging bumper, static, patient. Alex, as always, zigzagged, in and out of the frozen motorcade as though weaving a thread of exhaust fumes around them, looking back at us and laughing, kicking his legs out stiffly and nearly hitting the wall. Jonathon looked over his shoulder, opened the throttle and we whistled past all the cars, plus Alex who was now stopped beside a car, arguing with a petulant motorist. We reached Cobham and rode once more along the seafront, looking at the mighty, calm, glittering seas beside us, and the wandering, pondering crowds of holidaymakers who relished days like this; all those sun-reddened, skin-peeling foreigners with their city dialects and sulking daughters, dark glasses and tar-covered feet. We sped around the small car park and out along the seafront yet again. I was beginning to relax. Jonathon was quite a safe rider really, as long as he didn't go fast. I was glad I was with him and not with Alex. No matter who I was riding pillion with, though, I could never get the hang of leaning over when taking corners. I was always petrified of the laws of gravity suddenly tugging me to the hard, flesh-tearing ground, ripping me apart like a cheese-grater and scattering the bits all over the road. Yeah, I was full of morbid visions, riding pillion.

Alex, our arrantly reckless companion, caught up with us, still in bottom gear by the sound of his screaming engine. His loose parka was flapping tightly back from his body, his hair whipped and ruffled by the wind, his long legs protruding from behind the leg-shield. He rode level with us and looked quickly over.

'You fancy going into the Lobster Pot for a coffee?'

'Yeah,' I shouted back. I could have done with a drink.

Just then I heard the rumble of a motorcycle behind us. I stretched myself up and looked behind me. My heart twanged when I recognised the helmeted face. It was Clive, Mary's old boyfriend. I instantly turned back in my seat hoping that he didn't see me, or remember me. I didn't want a continuation of the scrap we had at the fair that time. He was bound to bear a grudge. I felt sure he wouldn't dare do anything with Jonathon and Alex with me, though. He came level with us, his motorcycle roaring powerfully, looking straight ahead of him, ignoring us, intent on just overtaking us and going on his way, I think. To my horror, Alex started making faces at him. Clive looked down at him and sneered in distaste.

'Why. Look at these little moddy-boys on their kiddy-machines. What's it like to have top speed of five miles an hour then, jerks?'

He changed gear with a click and swerving around a dog, leaving us as though we were stationary, fixed like glue on the road, amidst his fumes, and dust. I grabbed hold of the back-rack in a panic as Jonathon suddenly slammed into lower gear and gave chase.

I broke out in a cold sweat as Jonathon shot past a surprised Alex and a horn-blaring car. The wind was tearing through my hair like icy fingers. I stretched myself over Jonathon's broad shoulders to see how far we were behind Clive, shouting into his ear.

'Hey...just slow down will....will ya?'

Christ, I wanted to get off, to be safe and secure on solid, motionless ground. This motorcycle chasing was mindless and dangerous. I went rigid as we leaned right over to take a corner, the running board scraping the surface of the road, spraying sparks into the air like a sparkler firework.

'Can't we just forget it..?' I screamed into Jonathon's ear as we straightened up again. 'Just stop, can't you...please?'

I could hear Alex's voice, shouting and yelping behind.

'Go on, Jonathon. You can do it. Overtake the bastard.'

I stretched myself over Jonathon's shoulders again, my mind reeling in a frenzied mania. Clive was looking back at us, wobbling slightly, not that far ahead of us, then turning back hunched over his handle bars, flapping his back wheel like a huge metal fish, taunting us, enticing my friend to go still faster.

Jonathon wrenched back his throttle and we thrust even faster through the screaming air. Everything around me seemed to be waxen, molten, streaming, melted, whirling, the fleeting houses, shouting children, trotting dogs, staring people in doorways, whooshing cars, blurring past...rushing past...rushing...the air blasting into my face...

I could hear Jonathon's screaming voice.

'We're going to do it...overtake...overtake the bastard...'

Tears caused by the wind were running down his cheek from his eyes and blowing on to my face. I could hear Alex's trill, triumphant shrieking behind me, the wild engine between my legs rattling and vibrating so highly pitched I felt sure it would explode.

'Go one Jonathon...I'm right behind you...go on...you can do it...'

From nowhere, seemingly, a car shot out in front of us. I grabbed Jonathon's shoulders in a panic, clawing into his flesh as he stamped his foot on the brake, his whole body suddenly taut, stiff, wrenching the handlebars sharply to the left, swearing loudly. The car's silver-grilled front leered up to us with a screeching of brakes. We cut off almost at a right angle, leaning over dangerously, the front tyre scuffing sideways across the hot tarmac.

The car hit our back-rack with a crack and a snapping of metal, its headlights splattering into a shattered mosaic. We went sliding, over-balanced, crazily across the road, scattering sparks and glass into the humming air, shedding a side-panel that went spinning up silently like space debris, returning to the ground with a buckling clatter. I collided with the hard surface of the road, torn from my seat, rolling, numbed, seeing the rapid sight of the scooter, and Jonathon, still skimming on its side across the road, like a flat pebble across water, then resting against a grass bank, its wheels still spinning. My body scraped along the surface of the road, then stopped, my feet pressing against the kerb, my arms stretched above me, my face kissing the tarmac, pain suddenly racking me like a feverish orgasm. I lay for a few minutes only. Then I heard Alex's scooter wobble uncontrollably past me, just missing my hair. I lifted my head as though in a drunken stupor, and saw him bouncing over the pavement like a pogo stick, his legs kicking out, then careering right over into a flower bed....crash. Although none of us were hurt too much, it implanted in me a relentless awareness of the danger of riding pillion on a fast scooter, but it didn't change Alex. I'd still see him, his hair struck back from his forehead by the wind, his arms straight and taut, his body leaning back, riding his scooter down some steep hill, his face contorted with a grimace, half-expecting to either kill himself, or anyone who got in the way.

144

Chapter 17

One day, without surprise, he found himself again with no money, with empty pockets, no cigarettes and no wit. He took off all the chromium accessories from his scooter and sold them, having, then, enough money to last another week. But the state of Alex's scooter was getting increasingly pitiful. The once-glossy sheen of its bodywork had been eaten away by a rusty cancerous growth giving it the appearance of a brown-and-red-bleeding motivated heap of scrap. Then one day, the thing stopped. Alex took his scooter to our local mechanic who had a dark cluttered shed at the back of the trading estate. He was the sort of man who seemed to be forever working, even until midnight sometimes, working on dismantled engines by the light of a bare light bulb, his transistor radio perched on the work bench, tuned to Radio Luxembourg. He had worked on all our scooters at one time or another. He even let us take them away, after being repaired, without paying the bill. Everyone owed him money. Rumour had it, though, that he was a heavy drinker, and only worked so hard because his wife wouldn't let him in the house. His shed was certainly full of scooters he hadn't begun to work on yet, the corners piled high with old engines and empty oil cans.

He had some pretty grim habits, too. Screaming at awkward nuts he couldn't undo, and calling them crude, abbreviated names of the female anatomy was acceptable, but he did tend, quite unexpectedly, to suddenly open his flies and start urinating on the workshop floor when you were talking to him, or pick his nose and rub the contents on his leg, or break wind. You couldn't take a girl to see him. Although he was the most popular, and cheapest mechanic in town, he had a thing about scooters...he hated them.

'Bloody women's machines,' he'd call them. 'Why don't you get a good Triumph?' he'd advise us. 'I can get you one for a good price...Christ. If I'd have been seen on one of them scooter things in my youth I'd have been laughed off the surface of the earth....'

'It's the Permissive Society,' Alex would tell him, somewhat impatiently.

So it was in this mechanic's hands, oily adamant, with that dogmatic opinion and heavy-breathing inebriety, that the end came for Alex. The scooter was left in the workshop for over six months and during that passing time he had grown into other things. He even bought a Mini van, painted it, failed the driving test, and left it in his garage. He worked through different jobs, still stayed infatuated with Vanessa, started rolling his own cigarettes, still got drunk, but now he was meeting new friends, and wasn't talking about scooters so much. In the end, the scooter was finally repaired, but it was no longer taxed or insured. Alex pushed it home and left it in the garage with the van he still could not afford to run, or drive. Parked there, neglected, forgotten, rusted and silent, it remained.

Part IV

Summer

Well fare thee well
You know I got to ramble
And where I'm bound
I cannot say
Along that misty road that leads to nowhere
You know I got to go away
You know I got to go away

Chapter 18

With the annual summer came the warm breezes, the hot pavements, the attraction to sun-tanned girls, the distant hills alive with insects and ablaze with flowers, and the bees like miniature flying buffalos. The poetry of sunshine and contentment thawed and eased our frozen, wintered minds. The summer always seemed to cause an anti-magnetic breaking apart of the numbers and way of life. The Youth Club was closed down from June to October, and even our urban haunts were deserted and avoided during these months. No longer would we meet around the old drinks machine in the car park, or queue together along the aluminium counter in the fish and chip shop. No more the well worn groove, set sequence of Monday picture night. All order and pre-arranged plans were either forgotten, or refused. We were as scattered, during the hot summer months, as honey bees from the hive.

We were lucky being so near the sea. A three mile ride and we'd be there: Cobham, with its pebbled beaches, its gently pulsating mass of cool sea, with the screeching of seagulls in the golden sky above, and the multitudes, the summer tides of holiday-making girls we promised to meet, and take out. Tee-shirts and jeans were the order of the day, but we didn't discard our parkas. We took the linings out so they were lighter and cooler, though they then looked even scruffier and flimsier. We washed our scooters and piled on the chrome. The way to a summer girl's heart, we thought, was through her admiration for untidy boys on heaped-up scooters embellished with silver bars and covered with stickers and paint.

Indeed, we did arrange a meeting place in Cobham where we could all meet and arrange a routine for that evening, but our plans were never adhered to, and we would wander off in pairs, or ride up to the seafront on our own to bask in the hazy sunlight, or sit on the small wall licking ice-cream, or eating hamburgers. The telegraph pole beside the river became our new meeting place, though it was neither discovered nor arranged; it was just accepted and that was that. So one summer evening only three of us were parked and waiting beside that telegraph pole: Owen, Alex and I. Owen leaned back on his backrest and closed his eyes as the sun hit him in the face. I sat on my running boards smoking. Alex was feasting hungrily on a hamburger, making a loud mumbling noise and rolling his eyes, pretending he hadn't eaten for days.

Around the corner Raymond came gliding smoothly on his three-month old GP, his backrest packed high with blankets and dangling saucepans. He reached us in a whisper of dust, smelling of polish, clean rubber and newly run-in engine. He pulled his scooter up on to its stand and sat there, sunglasses over his eyes, a thin chequered scarf around his neck and his immense parka billowing slightly with a breeze.

'Don't tell us. Let's guess,' said Alex, dryly, 'you're off for the weekend.'

'That's right,' he replied, nodding slowly.

'Where are you going this time?' asked Owen, admiring his scooter, so thickly polished he could see a glossily-contorted, mutated reflection of himself, like gazing into a crazy mirror in a fun-parlour.

'Land's End,' said Raymond proudly.

'When are you going?' asked Alex, not really that interested.

150

Raymond started his scooter with a single prod of his heel, shifted into gear with a slight motion of his fist, then pushed himself forward off the stand, sinking and rising slightly as a boat would, if cushioned by its tyres and adequate suspension.

'I am now gone,' he said and he suddenly sped up the street, waving quickly, leaving us a tiny blue puff of exhaust smoke, and was, indeed gone.

'Goodbye,' said Alex.

'He never told us he was going to Land's End,' I said.

Alex finished his hamburger.

'What are we going to do?'

'Fancy a drink?' said Owen.

'You buying me one?' asked Alex.

'I will,' I said, standing, 'let's go.'

We walked up to the Lobster Pot on the seafront and found it crowded with holiday-makers, thick with a fug of cigarette smoke, and noisy. We worked our way to the bar, bought our drinks and found a place to sit down. A jump-suited man with a red electric guitar was strumming some block chords and singing with a slurred voice, hunched on a stool on a tiny stage. Halfway through a rendition of *Take Me Home County Roads,* I noticed the juke box was still switched on. I walked over and selected some records. We waited and sniggered into our glasses when we watched the singer trying to compete with *Pinball Wizard*. The manager came over and told us to "watch it", and promptly turned the juke box off. Owen went to get us some more drinks. Alex prodded my elbow.

'Jack,' he said, 'see what I see?'

I looked across the crowded bar. Two young girls, bare-shouldered and healthily tanned were looking our way and whispering.

'What do you think?' I said.

'I like mine. I'm not sure about yours, though,' he replied.

'I like the one with the black curly hair.'

'Me too.'

Owen returned and handed us our drinks.

'Come on,' said Alex, 'let's go over there.'

'Hang on,' I said, flustered, 'not so fast. We've got to plan these things out. Haven't we?'

We sat and thought a while, sipping our beers. The girls were still looking at us.

'Look,' said Alex, 'they're obviously interested. They've been giving us the eye for the last bloody five minutes. So we're going over there. Alright?'

'What are we going to say?' I croaked.

He downed his beer and sighed heavily.

'Christ,' he said, 'do I have to tell you everything?'

We all stood up, but then he suddenly froze and grabbed my arm.

'Yeah. Perhaps it is a little hasty', he said losing his bravado slightly.

'C'mon,' said Owen, laughing at us, 'we'll make with the Mister Smoothies.'

We made our way across the crowded bar. My heart began to thump wondering what on earth I was going to say to these girls we had never met before. I was sure to show myself up with my fumbling, nervous inadequacies.

We reached their table and stood there. I was smirking miserably, trying to hide behind Alex.

'May we join you?' said Owen.

The two girls moved up, giving us room to sit down. Alex and Owen sat beside them. I grabbed an empty chair and pulled it to the table and sat opposite, crossing my legs and looking at my plimsolls. How I wished I was pissed, then I wouldn't have cared what they thought of me. I could smell their perfume wafting into my nostrils.

'On holiday?' Alex asked them.

The girls giggled.

'My name's Alex,' he said, 'and this is Owen, and Jack.'

They looked at me and smiled.

'We...well,' I began, 'we thought we'd come over and....uh...y'know....uh.'

The girl I was watching shrugged her slender shoulders and grinned.

'Um. Yes. Thank you, Jack,' said Alex

'What do you do around here?' said the other girl, with hair like a mass of tiny spikes, 'is this place all there is?'

'There's a disco every Saturday,' Owen told her.

'Upstairs,' I said, pointing a finger to the ceiling, 'they have it in the ballroom upstairs.'

'Anyway. What are your names?' Alex asked them.

'My name's Carol,' said the one with the spikes, 'and her name's Jill.'

Jill nodded her head, then blew a smoke ring from her opened mouth and it drifted slowly and dreamily across the table like a suspended, phantom doughnut.

'Wow,' I cried, impressed, 'that was good. How d'you do that?'

'We're both pretty fed up,' said Carol looking at Owen, 'there's nothing to do around here.'

'It's pretty easy,' Jill told me,'...just needs practice.'

I brought out my cigarette packet.

'Ah. Give me a fag will ya, Jack?' said Alex and he pulled one from the packet. I offered the others around. Owen and Carol declined so Alex and I both lit up.

'I wonder if I can do it?' I said, inhaling deeply. 'Blow a smoke ring.'

Carol finished drinking her bitter lemon.

'How about going for a ride somewhere, then?' Owen asked. 'It's quite a nice evening.'

The girls looked at each other, thinking deeply and grinning.

'Yes. OK,' said Carol, finally, 'why not?'

I made to stand up. I'd leave them to it, I decided, seeing as they were paired off. I'd walk down to my scooter and ride into town, I thought.

'What kind of car do you have?' Jill asked me suddenly, leaning across the table and blinking her wide, brown eyes.

'Car?' I said, looking over at Alex, flustered, 'car?'

'Car?' said Owen, taken aback.

'Alright, alright, "car" she says,' said Alex, flushing with embarrassment, 'what's the big deal?'

'We don't have cars,' Owen explained to the girls. 'We ride scooters, we're moddies.'

Alex grimaced. They burst into a sudden paroxysm of laughter, snorting, grabbing each other and hitting the table with their hands. We sat stunned while Alex looked away, trying to appear unperturbed. Carol stopped laughing briefly, still teary-eyed.

'I don't think so...' she said, then choked with laughter again. 'Thanks anyway...'

We stood up and walked towards the door.

'Well done, Mister Smoothy,' said Alex.

Chapter 19

Sundays always depressed me. The town was always so empty, so desolate and lonely; a sheer wasteland, with so many silent streets and bolted doors. I nearly always woke too early, couldn't get back to sleep, and ended up riding around the town or sitting alone in the Café Majestic. Mary was still constantly on my mind. I just couldn't forget her. I hadn't seen her for over six months, and I wondered where she was, and what she was doing, who she was with, and why she didn't come out anymore. Was she married, or dead? I rode once more up the deserted street and decided to buy a cup of coffee. The Café Majestic had only just opened so I had to hang about by the counter while the espresso machine was switched on and refilled. In the end I decided to have a glass of milk instead. I went over to the window and sat down. I lit a cigarette. I sipped my milk. I looked over at the seats where Mary and I had sat many months ago. I remembered the times she used to wait for me patiently when I worked here. Christ. I remembered so many things about her.

Mary was forever, constantly on my mind. As I was now working as a groundsman on the golf links at Cobham, this gave me ample time to think... just of Mary. I'd drive the tractor thinking of her, lean on the lawn mower thinking of her, forever thinking... mesmerised by memories. I'd even wake from a short, fitful night's sleep feeling depressed, then wonder why, then remember, remember Mary, then feel the depression press down upon me almost unbearable. I was boring my friends by talking about her so much. No-one could do anything to help me. I was just tiring my friends' ears with my constant rapping about the same thing. I thought I might die of heartache. I'd even ride past her bungalow at night, and sometimes park in the darkness and just stare at her bedroom window, tearing myself apart just thinking about her. Every record I heard was about her. No other girl was like her. Christ. I was screwing myself up so tightly, I was bleeding dry.

My train of thought was broken by the sound of a scooter coming into the car park. I looked through the large window and saw Owen ride once around, then see me and wave. He rode across and parked outside the window, beside the wall. He waved again, then walked into the cafeteria, bought a coffee, came over, and sat next to me. I was really pleased to see someone so early on a Sunday morning.

'How's it going?' he asked.

'OK,' I said, 'I guess.'

He sipped his coffee.

'What's wrong then?'

'Same thing.'

He seemed mildly surprised.

'What. You still hung up over that girl?'

I liked Owen. He always seemed to be interested in other people's problems. He was always helping out mending our scooters or giving us lifts home when we were really stuck. I couldn't understand why he always wore a suit, though. It wasn't a new, nicely-pressed, smart suit he wore, but some old really, crumpled, almost-shiny, untidy apparel that always made him look bedraggled, like a party-goer lost in the desert. That was his only bad point. It was probably to do with the fact that he wanted to become a civil servant. He always wore a parka though, which was a relief.

'What's her name again?'

I paused. 'Mary. Mary Hawker,' I told him. Even speaking her name hurt sometimes.

He sipped his coffee, loudly.

'I saw her just now,' he said.

My heart suddenly banged.

'You saw her? Where?'

'She was walking down the street with her sister. Heading this way.'

'Christ,' I said, feeling my face burning, and my hands trembling. 'I haven't seen her for months.'

'She'll probably be coming in here,' Owen surmised.

'Christ. What am I going to do?' I said in a panic.

'I'd just forget her, Jack,' Owen advised me. 'I've heard all about her. She's no good. You could find a really nice chick.'

Owen didn't really know my head, how obsessed I was with thoughts of Mary, my helplessness, my frantic state of mind. I wished I hadn't seen him now. Still, I was glad he told me he had seen her coming down the street. If I had bumped into her on my way out or something, I might have died of shock. I was very immature about such things.

'How are you getting on with your new job?' Owen asked, wanting to change the subject.

'It's OK,' I told him, trying to concentrate on what I was saying. 'I cut grass all day, and rake sand bunkers, healthy...outdoors...in the sunshine, y'know.'

'Sounds alright.'

I crushed my cigarette in the ashtray, then lit another. I heard the cafeteria doors sigh open, pause, then close again with a rush of air. I heard heels walking towards the counter. Owen looked at me.

'They've just walked in,' he told me.

I looked across the empty café and saw Mary and her sister pushing into each other and giggling, making their way along the self-service counter. My face was burning so much that I felt it might melt. Like candle-wax, and drip in little droplets on the table.

'You're blushing, Jack,' Owen informed me, grinning.

'Shit,' I whispered between my teeth.

I looked over again at the sisters waiting to be served. Mary had had her hair cut and it was really short. I hadn't seen her for so long it was like seeing her for the first time. A feeling of desire and affection flushed over me. She turned her head and saw me. I looked away quickly.

'Shall I go over and ask them to come and sit with us? Owen suggested.

I grabbed his parka sleeve in a sudden fright. 'No, Christ. No don't you dare.'

'I just thought...' he began.

'I couldn't handle it,' I explained.

I picked up my glass of milk and my hand was shaking really badly, quite uncontrollably. The glass suddenly slipped through my fingers and landed with a deafening crack on the table, spitting milk all over my parka, then rolled off onto the floor with a tinkling explosion.

'Shit and hell,' I spat through my teeth leaning over the edge of the table, seeing the shards of glass scattered over the tiled floor.

'You are in a state,' said Owen, calmly. 'I'll go and ask for a dustpan and brush.'

I hid my tingling face behind my hands and stared blindly through the window. Why was I always so bloody uncool? I was always showing myself up. Christ. How I hated myself.

I heard Mary's voice from across the café. I looked over briefly and saw her colliding playfully with Owen, pretending to be knocked backwards. Owen helped her to stand straight and she pressed her body tightly against his, whispering something into his ear. That girl would flirt with anyone, anywhere. I hated Owen for that instant, too, for being so close to the girl I loved, when all I could do was show myself up in front of her. Mary rejoined her sister at the counter and they bought their cups of coffee, then made their way towards me. Mary was wearing a knee-length skirt and a pair of brown leather boots that reached just under her knees. I had never seen her in a skirt before and she looked quite a smart young woman. She could wear anything well. I always thought leather boots were sexy, but seeing them on Mary, they were verging on the erotic. I stared through the window hearing Mary's heels drawing nearer and nearer, screwing up my eyes. She came so close I felt she was going to sit right down next to me. I could even smell her, smell that same perfume she always used to use. She seemed to pause there, above me, and I was too afraid to look up at her or say hello because I knew my face was as brightly-red as a traffic light.

'Come on, Mary,' said her sister's voice, suddenly, 'let's sit over there...Hello Jack.'

They walked over to the corner behind me. I looked over my shoulder.

'Uh...hi...uh...Jennifer...alright?' I blurted, weakly.

Owen returned with a dustpan and started brushing up the fragments of glass.

'You've got to pay for the glass,' he told me, hunkered down, brushing there, 'they just told me.'

'What did she say to you just then?' I whispered at him.

'The guy behind the counter just said...'

'I'm talking about Mary,' I rasped, sharply, 'when she spoke to you, just then...'

He placed the dustpan and brush on a nearby table and sat down opposite me again, looking over my shoulder at the two girls in the corner.

'She just told me to tell you to behave yourself,' he told me amused.

'She told you that?' I said, surprised.

'She's looking over at you right now,' he said, suddenly sounding confidential and soft, crouching low.

'Thrills,' I said, trying to act cool and unmoved, though the flags were flying in my head, feeling that, perhaps, Mary still liked me after all this time.

'Why don't you go over and talk to her?' he asked.

'Christ. I can't,' I said, 'it's not as easy as that.'

Owen didn't understand things. He couldn't understand why I didn't just go over there and sit next to her if I liked her that much. I could just see myself doing that though: walking over all cool and confident, and she thinking "what's that prat coming over here for?" then me suddenly tripping over my plimsoll lace or something, crashing to the floor, writhing and squirming on those tiles, and she there sipping her quiet coffee, watching me. Sure, I could see it all; me twisting and tangling on that chequered surface like a manic silverfish, unable to stand, and Mary getting up very slowly and walking all over me like a doormat, rubbing the dirt off the soles of those sexy boots, all over my....Christ. Why was I always so full of raving fantasies?

'Hey,' said Owen, sitting up, 'her sister's coming over.'

'What? Over here?'

160

I froze, my heart thumping in my chest, waiting, breathing slowly, hearing her shoes on the tiles, then her voice.

'Jack.'

I looked around and saw Jennifer, her lips shining with glossy lipstick, her hair longer than when I last saw it, her eyelids carefully and lightly mascaraed, looking pretty and serious, both at the same time.

'Hello, Jennifer,' I said, 'how are you?' Alright?'

She pulled out a chair from the opposite table and sat down, studying the ketchup bottle.

'Mary wants to speak to you,' she said.

I took a quick look across at Mary and saw her staring at me. 'What does she want?' I asked, looking at Jennifer again, trying to hold back a broad smile. Wow. This was more like it. She must have felt something for me, after all this time, and she was making the first move.

'Come on over and find out,' said Jennifer, standing, 'OK?' she's waiting.'

She started walking back to her place in the corner.

'I'll think about it,' I called, loud enough for Mary to hear. Although I was dying to go over there, I had to play it cool.

'There you are,' said Owen, knocking back his dregs of coffee, 'she fancies you again. Are you going to go over there?'

'I might do.'

I suppose now he was wondering why I didn't run over there straight away. I don't know. After all these months of fretting and pining over Mary, now that I could be with her, I wanted to give her the impression that I was indifferent and couldn't care less. It was all to do with my pride.

'I'm going to get another coffee,' Owen said, standing, 'you want one?'

'Yeah, thanks. And ask them how much they want me to pay for that glass.'

'It shouldn't be more than about twenty pee,' he suggested. He took the dustpan from the table and walked across the cafeteria. I stubbed out my cigarette. I looked at my scooter parked near the wall. I looked up at the clock on the wall. It was nearly ten o'clock. I heard Mary's voice behind me arguing with her sister. I listened carefully and heard my name mentioned several times. I even thought I heard Mary crying, sobbing, murmuring, very quietly. I decided to wait another minute or so, long enough to make her think I wasn't going over, then breeze across, all calm and nonchalant, almost blasé, like.

I heard the sudden scraping of chairs, then the rapid click-clack click-clack of heels coming towards me. I looked up and gaped, holding my breath. Mary was there, like a sudden apparition, looking straight down at me, her eyes red with crying, her arms folded across her breast, shivering.

'Aren't you talking to me, then?' she asked, sniffing.

'I...I was...just about to come over to see you,' I stammered, feeling my face and neck burning again.

'Can I sit down?'

'Yeah....,' I said, moving my chair up a bit. 'Sure.'

She sat beside me, moving her chair closer so our shoulders were touching.

'I haven't seen you for a long time,' she said, pulling a handkerchief from a pocket on her skirt, still sniffing, then blowing her nose.

'No, that's right,' I agreed, placing my hands between my knees so she wouldn't see them shaking, remembering all at once that I had "Jack and Mary"

162

scribbled in indelible biro all over the front of my parka. 'What have you been getting up to?'

I couldn't believe that she was really there; so close, so real, so palpable. It was like one of my many daydreams of her suddenly flashing into reality. It had all happened so quickly.

'You wouldn't believe me,' she said, still sniffing, stuffing her handkerchief back into her skirt pocket, then attempting to make a sexy growl, only it was cut off by another involuntary sob.

She was forever trying to be the vulnerable, accessible sex bomb, wild, insatiable, but fragile. She never seemed to let up. She wasn't the best-looking girl in town, far from it; in fact a lot of my friends thought her plain but her relentless, helpless sex-pose always seemed to work for me. She always turned me on, no matter what she did. She could even wear an old potato sack and make it look sensual. There was just this provocative "something" about her. No-one felt the same way about her. Maybe I was perverted or something, seeing more in her than there really was. She certainly had a bad reputation among my friends, without having done anything. None of them would even consider going out with her. She went out with "greasers" anyway.

'Everyone I go out with is only interested in one thing,' she said, almost back to her normal self, as I looked at the table, 'they've all got one track minds; usually dirt-track ones.'

Jennifer appeared and sat opposite us, moving over the chair so she could sit by the window.

'You've got back together, then,' she surmised.

Mary wheeled her lighter alight and offered it to my cigarette. I lit up.

'I don't know about "getting back together",' I told her, spitting out a shred of tobacco that had stuck to my tongue, 'I've got to think about it yet.'

Owen returned and placed a cup of coffee in front of me.

'They want eighteen pence for the broken glass,' he said, sitting down next to Jennifer. Mary suddenly burst into tears, covering her face with her hands, the cigarette between her fingers trembling.

'Stroll on,' breathed Owen, stirring his coffee, 'what's wrong with *her*?'

'Now you've upset her again,' said Jennifer reaching over the table to comfort her sister. 'She's been wanting to see you for days. She keeps on talking about you at home. She wanted to apologise for the way she treated you, and all you do is make her cry...'

'He hates me,' Mary croaked, twisting sharply on her chair, turning her back to me.

I looked at Owen and he tutted, raising his eyebrows. I was quite enjoying myself. It was quite a thrill to see Mary making all this fuss, thinking I didn't like her any more. I sipped my coffee, gloating, considering how far I would go. Mary turned on her chair and looked at me morosely, her eyes half closed, tears dribbling down her cheeks, disarming me momentarily.

'I'll do anything for you,' she said.

'OK,' I replied, drawing on my cigarette, 'you can pay the eighteen pence I owe for that glass.'

She stood up instantly, silently, slim and curved, then squeezed past my chair and walked towards the counter.

'Aren't you mean,' said Owen, watching her cross the cafeteria.

'She likes you a hell of a lot,' Jennifer told me. 'Really.'

'I believe you,' I told her.

Mary returned and squeezed past my chair and sat beside me again.

'I did it,' she said, pressing her knees against me.

'Are you going to go out with her now?' asked Jennifer.

I pretended to contemplate, rubbing my chin.

'Uuuumm,' I paused. '....No.'

'You *bastard*,' Mary suddenly spat, standing erect, her chair screeching on the tiles, toppling backwards. She pushed past me, pressing at the back of my chair then half-ran, tripping, towards the door, her heels stuttering on the tiles.

'You're bloody rotten, you are,' Jennifer shouted at me, angrily. 'I'll never forgive you.'

The café door heaved open with a gasp of air, and Mary was gone.

'I didn't mean...' I gasped, befuddled, realising I had gone too far. 'I will go out with her. Go and tell her. Will you? Please?'

Jennifer stood up with a frown.

'Alright, but don't blame me if she doesn't want to see you again.'

She ran to the door. Mary appeared again, leaning against the wall, waiting for Jennifer, then turned to go.

'You do complicate your life, don't you?' Owen opined, moving his head from side to side in apparent wonderment.

'You're bloody right,' I agreed, sipping my coffee fiercely. I watched the girls talking outside the window, their voices muted by the thick glass, feeling desperate and afraid; just now she was crawling after me, now it was completely the other way around.

'How ever do you manage it?' said Owen sipping his coffee.

Jennifer returned.

'It's alright,' she said. 'Mary said you can take her home, if you want to.'

I stood in the car park, the cafeteria door closing slowly behind me, cushioned by its grasshopper-like hydraulic arm and currents of air. I looked at Mary, she came over and quietly took my arm. She had an expression of tired relief on her face.

'I've missed you,' she said. We walked to my scooter. I started it and mounted, she climbed on the back, grabbing my shoulders, then sat there wrapping her arms around my stomach. I sped across the car park knowing that Jennifer and Owen were watching me, watching me fall once more into that same tired trap...

Mary's family were in, so we went into the kitchen. She made me a cup of coffee and sat talking to me. I looked around me, taking in that familiar room, remembering its walls and furniture, its keen, kitcheny smells. I always thought I'd never see the place again. I had one of Mary's home-made cakes. It tasted incredibly dry. I looked at the clock and decided to go home for lunch. I arranged to pick her up again at seven o'clock that evening. She told me she was going to be busy that afternoon. I kissed her. At home I was so excited I couldn't eat my lunch, or my dinner. That evening I got smartened up in my best 501s, my blue Ben Sherman, and even splashed some Brut expensively all over my neck. I rode up the lane to Mary's bungalow beaming, enveloped in sheer contentment. It was dead on seven. I didn't dare be late. Going out with Mary was all I was living for. I knocked on the door. There was the barking of dogs. Jennifer answered the door, looking sorry for me.

'She had to go out and see someone,' she told me. 'She's already gone out...'

Chapter 20

It was so hot one lazy Saturday afternoon Alex and I went down to the beach, stripped off our shirts and just lay there, motionless, at peace, not saying a word, basking in the sun. The sea, so vast and calm that afternoon, lapped on the beach rinsing the pebbles with a swirling, foamy froth then it dragged back with a loud sucking noise. The ubiquitous, ever-present seagulls chattered and flew in circles in the blinding sky above us. A small fishing boat was dotted upon the distant horizon.

'It's lovely,' Alex mumbled, an arm over his eyes, though still attired in that ragged, paint-splattered tee-shirt, looking quite thin and wasted.

I sat up and looked along the beach. A few holiday-maker families were scattered along the shore with their large beach-umbrellas propped up like emaciated mushrooms, casting elliptical shadows on the pebbles. An old man was paddling, his trousers rolled up over his knees, a tiny dog splashing and yapping around him.

The beach stretched out along the edge of the sea for immeasurable miles then finally evaporated into a dreamy heat-shifting mist, somewhere near Baybridge. Cobham's two sleepy piers protruded into the gentle water like two concreted fingers. An assortment of fishermen, both young and old, were hunched upon the high walls, silhouetted against the huge yellow sun, their fishing lines like thin gossamer, their floats bobbing up and down on the water. I pushed my plimsolls off, pulled off my socks and stood up. Alex looked at me with one eye.

'What are you doing?'

'Going for a swim,' I told him.

167

I walked down to the heaving sea with difficulty. The large pebbles hurt my denuded feet and it was hard to keep my balance. A far-reaching wave slapped up to me, as green as glass, and covered my feet up to my ankles. It was cold and powerful but I pressed on until I was waist deep in the surging, dark, magic water. I stood there, the eddies moving around me, pulling me, causing me to almost topple over. I sprang forward, smashing head-on into an oncoming wave, holding my breath in the cold darkness, staying submerged until I arched up to the surface again, my stomach just skimming the pebbles, breaking once more into the sunlight, my hair wet in my face, gasping for breath. I swam around clumsily for a while then decided to get back on the beach.

My jeans were wet and heavy and clung to my legs, and a sudden breeze made me shudder. When I reached Alex again, I noticed that he had been joined by Raymond and Matthew, with two girls wearing "kiss me quick" hats and frosty expressions. They must have seen our scooters parked by the beach and decided to walk along the beach to be with us. They watched me as I sat down, cold and shivering. I dried myself with my shirt.

'I didn't even know he could swim,' said Raymond.

'He's full of miracles,' said Alex.

Matthew shucked off his parka and laid it out on the beach, then he and the girl sat down and immediately started kissing, she patting her hat to prevent it falling off her head as their faces moved slowly together, like slightly repelling magnets. Alex lay there grinning, shielding his eyes from the sunlight with his arm. Raymond remained standing, his arm around the other girl's shoulders, the badges on his parka winking and flashing like glitter. 'Are any of you going to the barn dance tonight?' he said.

'What time?' I asked, now feeling warmer, tingling with vitality and freshness.

'Nine o'clock.'

'No doubt we'll find our way there,' said Alex.

We left the beach just as the sun was sinking beyond the sea. By eight o'clock we were together again; all washed and changed and waiting around the inevitable telegraph pole. There were twenty of us that evening; quite a good number. We started our scooters and made our noisy way up the street. Some of us were wearing suits. Not me, though. I didn't have one. I just put on a clean shirt. A mile further into the country we stopped and crowded into a pub for a drink. When we came out, an hour later, nearly all of us were drunk. We travelled on, speeding past the rustling hedges and gently sighing trees, passing the lumbering, undulating, brown and green pied fields that stretched beyond us, for another three miles when the sound of a rock band reached our ears on a gentle breeze.

We parked our scooters together under some trees then stood around lighting cigarettes and figuring how we could get into the dance without paying.

'If we climb over that wall,' said Alex, pointing, 'we could run across the field, hide behind the bogs, then quietly nip into the barn. Easy.'

'Yeah but what if the bouncers get us? They usually have really heavy bastards here,' said Owen, looking worried. 'I'm not getting my suit crumpled for the sake of fifty pee, or whatever it is.'

'Puh,' Alex snorted, folding his arms across his chest, 'what do you mean, "if the bouncers catch us?" The bouncers aren't going "to catch us".'

'Well, I'm not clambering over no wall,' said Raymond, wearing a really sharp, well-fitted brown suit, 'I've got my best threads on.'

'You big smoothie you,' said Alex, looking him up and down in disgust.

He did look pretty smart, though, I have to admit.

'I'm going to pay,' said Jonathon, suddenly walking off. He always did as he wanted. The bouncers didn't scare him, but no doubt, the idea of creeping around the darkening field like a load of commandos just didn't appeal to him. A few others followed after him.

'Killjoys,' said Alex sharply, watching their departure with an air of displeasure.

'I'll do it with you, Alex,' I told him.

He suddenly looked enthusiastic again.

'Well done Jack,' he said, then tossing away his cigarette, 'you and me are the only true Mods in this town.'

'See ya later on, then,' said Raymond walking off, then as an afterthought called back, 'bet you don't do it.'

Alex suddenly punched me lightly on the arm.

'C'mon Jack, let's show them.'

He walked over to his scooter, heaved it from its stand then pushed it over to the wall, then he pulled it back on to its stand again. He climbed on to the saddle, losing his balance slightly. He straightened up, reaching to the top of the wall. He was tall enough to look over. He suddenly ducked down again.

'There's somebody walking across the field,' he whispered across at me, 'we'd better wait a bit.'

I leant against the wall as Alex stood perched on his saddle with a puzzled look on his face. He then giggled as our eyes met. He peeped over the wall again and quickly jerked his head.

'Yeah. Quickly. It's all clear.'

He bent his knees then sprang up, grunting, levering himself up by his elbows, his right leg swinging upward in an arc, his foot twisting over the top of the wall. He heaved himself up so that he was lying right along the wall, then letting his leg over so that he was riding the wall like a horse. He looked quickly down at me.

'Follow right after me. OK?'

I nodded. He scrambled over and dripped like a cat down the opposite side of the wall. I heard him fall heavily on to the grass with a yelp, then pause.

'C'mon Jack. Hurry.'

I stood on the scooter saddle, heaved myself up like Alex, and kicked my leg up so that I was lying along the wall. I saw Alex crouching below me.

'Hurry up,' he rasped, shaking his head, 'for Chrissakes.'

'Alright, alright,' I whispered back at him irritably, 'give me a chance.'

I looked down. It was about ten feet to the ground. I was a lot higher than I thought I would be. I suddenly realised that I was pretty prominent there, up in the sky, with all those crowds of people not far away. I could hear the band playing Johnny B. Goode and the sound of girls laughing and men shouting in the distance.

'Let yourself down slowly,' said Alex softly, 'mind I'll grab your legs.'

The thought of me being suddenly grabbed by the scruff of the neck and pulled to the exit door by a bored, half-pissed, muscle-bound bouncer made me forget the distance between me and the grass momentarily and I swung myself over the top of the wall and eased myself down fretfully. I felt Alex grab my legs. I released my hold from the top of the wall and

171

we both tumbled to the dew-wet grass. Alex scrambled over to me instantly.

'Thank Christ for that,' he looked at me seriously, 'you alright?'

'Sure,' I breathed, trembling.

He grabbed my arm.

'Right, We'll both make a run for the back of the bogs over there, OK?'

I nodded and his face broke into a smile.

'Yaaah, Jack. We're gonna do it. Alright? We're gonna show the rest of those ass-holes in there who the real ravers in this town are. Just you and me, as always...'

'Christ,' I said suddenly, 'I wonder if Mary's at this dance?'

Alex looked at me briefly then scanned the dark field with darting eyes.

'Look. Just give it a break will ya. Just enjoy yourself.'

He pointed to a small shed at the far end of the field.

'OK, you ready to run for it? Right. Go like hell till you get to the back of those bogs...'

We both sprang up and loped across the squelching, soggy grass, panting and giggling, our plimsolls splattering into puddles of mud and cow excrement. We reached the shed and hid behind it, hugging each other panting for breath, trying to keep from laughing.

'Yaaaah,' Alex breathed, his chest rising and falling rapidly. 'We're nearly there. We're going to do it.'

He moved along the shed and poked his head around the edge.

'Yeah,' he called across, 'we're in, all we've got to do is get across a courtyard and into the barn itself. We've gotten past the entrance table and the bouncers and *all* those shits.'

I moved along the back of the shed and poked my head around. I saw a large courtyard crowded with people drinking and talking, eating hot dogs, sitting around on bales of hay, standing under coloured bulbs strung across the air, talking amidst the loud music coming from the dark barn.

'Yeah,' I agreed, 'just across the courtyard...'

'You're gonna be cool, OK?' Alex told me.

'What d'you mean?'

'Just act natural, OK? And if anyone wants to see your ticket you've lost it. Just walk on through. They'll think we've been in the bog.'

'OK...OK,' I said impatiently, 'I can handle it...'

'C'mon then,' he said looking across the courtyard and stepping out into the open, looking instantly natural, as though he had been in the dance all night. I followed after him and we made our way across the crowed courtyard, excusing our way through the drinking, jostling people. Then we were in the barn.

The band was really quite loud but also very good. The lead guitarist was playing a fast lead break, the fingers of his left hand dancing delicately up and down the fretboard like a spider on an electric grid, his head bowed, hair covering his face. He then tossed his head back, his hair falling around his sallow face like curtains, looking as though he was having an orgasm, eyes closed, body stilled, one arm in the air as his guitar screamed with feed-back sounding like a monotone siren. We reached the bar at the far end of the barn but had to wait ages to be served. The place was as congested and stifling as it could possibly have been without causing mass suffocation or manic nausea. Alex finally got served and handed me a pint of bitter. I saw Jonathon standing by the wall watching the band so

I went over to join him, spilling my drink slightly as someone pushed me.

'You two got in, then,' Matthew shouted above the music to me.

I nodded proudly and sipped my beer.

The band finished a number and there was a slight crackle of applause, then a mumbling of voices, then the band tore into *Route 66*, making me want to dance; only there was no room on the dance floor. Raymond and Owen fought through the crowd to join us. They had already picked up a couple of girls. It never took them long. They were quite nice too, both wearing jeans, of course, and these smock-top things, which was the new craze, apparently. They looked sort of pregnant in those smocks; pregnant without the swollen belly, if you know what I mean. Quite a few girls were wearing them at the dance. Fashion ideas spread like a disease in our area. The two girls looked me up and down as Raymond and Owen held them around their shoulders, watching the band. They made me feel quite embarrassed, actually, just looking at me and chewing gum. So I gave them both a smile and they smiled back and giggled. They probably thought I was great, coming from the town and riding a scooter and all. They were only country girls y'see. I bet I could have picked up a girl if I had wanted to, only I was shit-scared of being turned down and made a fool.

I was beginning to feel pretty pissed, what with the drinks we had on the way there and the pint I was drinking. I looked around me at the heaving rabble on the dance floor, all crushed there dancing and jostling around. A real jerkish couple were jiving, spinning around and grabbing each other's hands; all that stuff, like I saw once in an Adam Faith movie yonks ago. The film bored the ass off me but it showed all these chicks in bobby socks and pony tails doing this dance with these guys in tight jeans and skinny ties. Jiving like this couple. They looked about thirty and were obviously trying to look young. I couldn't bear to watch them. They looked just bloody stupid. Everyone looked totally out of it. A crowd of freaks in the corner were tossing their heads around, loping back and forth like demented gorillas, getting really into the music. They looked real raving lunatics there. Their chicks looked pretty nice though with hair all frizzled out and beads and long skirts and all. They were too old for me though. I wasn't into "hippy chicks", anyway with all that 'peace and love, man' crap.

That was the good thing about getting pissed. I could really appreciate things. Like, one of the things that turned me on about girls was if they could dance well. They may have been the plainest looking women on earth but if they could move well....Christ, I could almost fall in love with them. There were two girls dancing not far from me and I watched them, almost mesmerised. They were such beautiful movers. I really wanted to dance with them. I put my drink on the floor by the wall.

'What are you doing?' Jonathon asked me.

'I'm going to dance with those chicks,' I told him, pointing, 'see them?'

'Hang on then,' he said, putting his glass down with mine, 'I'll join you.'

I felt really confident walking over with Jonathon. They wouldn't refuse dancing with me, with Jonathon right there with me, I thought.

The End

Lightning Source UK Ltd.
Milton Keynes UK
UKOW05f1035051114

241085UK00002B/9/P